OWL'S FAIR

OWL STAR WITCH MYSTERIES BOOK 2

LEANNE LEEDS

Owl's Fair
ISBN Paperback: 978-1-950505-49-4
Published by Badchen Publishing
14125 W State Highway 29
Suite B-203 119
Liberty Hill, TX 78642 USA

Copyright © 2021 by Leanne Leeds

For permissions contact: info@badchenpublishing.com

OWL'S FAIR

CHAPTER ONE

$\mathcal{A}$yla stared at me with a mixture of disapproval and teenage arrogance. "But I still don't get it." Her loud voice echoed in the small bathroom. "It's wrong."

Thirteen-year-old sisters have a remarkable ability. They can start a discussion off with a premise. A question you think (mistakenly) is genuine, so you answer them in patient, meticulous detail. At the end of that explanation, you realize it wasn't a question. You'd actually gotten roped into a circular debate in which your debate partner arrives right back where they started after all your effort—as if they hadn't heard a word you said.

"The reason the star card is the one that glows

is because Astraea turned into stars when she left the planet, so her energy is now star stuff," I explained for the second time, this time with brevity. "I know everyone thinks Astraea's the goddess on the Justice card. And you are right; that card glowing would be an absolutely logical card to glow," I agreed while brushing my hair. "But that's not the card that glows to tell me who needs my help. Because star stuff. Got it?"

"But it should be."

"But it's not."

"But it should be." Ayla's mouth was set in a determined frown. Her dissatisfied expression reminded me of a younger version of myself. "It doesn't make sense to have the star card be the one that glows. The star card represents renewed hope and faith, and being blessed by the universe," she explained (as if I, the least of witches, never had an opportunity to be familiar with tarot cards). "The justice card represents justice and fairness and law. So that card should be the one that glows. You're stopping a crime."

"You forget that Archie was a gift from the goddess Athena, Ayla," Althea, fifteen, said as she entered the bathroom. Pushing gently past Ayla, she smiled. "That is a blessing from the universe, and I think it must be why the star card is the one that glows. It's not just about justice." Althea settled on the closed toilet and leaned against the counter, elbows on the edge and chin in her hands. "It's about the renewed hope and faith that saving someone marked for death brings about. Entirely religious, clearly. The blessing is from the universe itself interceding on their behalf so they may live."

"Well, I wouldn't go that far," I muttered, brushing my hair out of my face. "I do need to point out I'm trying to get ready, and I don't need every sister in the bathroom with me. Maybe we can have this discussion another time?" I looked around the counter. "Can you hand me that lip gloss?" I pointed next to Ayla, and she handed me the tube.

"Lip gloss? Really?" Ami poked her head in the door. "Where are you going?"

"I have to run to the police station." I painted a light burgundy color on my lips. "Emma said there's some reporter that wants to do a puff piece about all the closed cold cases we've been working on."

Althea rolled her eyes. "You know they're just going to make a joke of the psychic stuff." She dropped her eyes. "Don't mention the goddess. I wouldn't want our beliefs denigrated in print by a non-believer."

"They're not my beliefs, so that won't be a problem."

"Who cares what they write as long as they spell the shop's name, right?" Ayla pointed out. "Don't forget to mention the shop. If you don't, Mom will lose it. Any press is good press, but free press is way better."

Ami tousled Ayla's hair and then turned back to me. "Breakfast is ready, by the way. I smell cinnamon, too," she announced. My three sisters immediately engaged in a spirited discussion regarding whether Aunt Gwennie had made pancakes or French toast—and which they were hoping for.

Another chipper, cheerful morning at Arden House.

I stared at myself in the mirror and noted the dark circles under my eyes. I looked as tired as I felt. Spending all day working at the shop or the police station, then all evening with my sisters…it was fun, but it was taxing in a way military work had never been. My lack of "me" time was showing.

This lack of privacy baloney was getting old.

My face flushed pink even though I hadn't

said it out loud. That sounded a little bitter, didn't it? Ungrateful. Like I didn't want to be here.

It wasn't that.

They were just…so much.

You would think that after fifteen years in the military, I would be used to a certain amount of communal interaction. A lot of it, in fact. And I was…or I thought I was. However, my fellow soldiers had far more respect for my privacy than my three younger sisters ever thought to show me.

I sighed as they continued their cheerful back and forth.

I knew I had no cause to complain. I was thirty-three years old and living back with my family. That family consisted of three much younger sisters—twenty, fifteen, and thirteen— and an aunt, and my mother. I should feel lucky there was a place for me to go after I was fired from the Ministry of Arcane Fugitives—oops, I'm sorry.

Laid off, not fired.

Apparently, you're only fired if you do something wrong.

If your entire department is kicked to the curb, it's a layoff.

Someone must explain the difference to me one day.

Either way, with my lifelong career (which came with room and board) in the latrine, I should be grateful I had a place to go. And I was.

Especially since my pension was still up in the air.

"Why do you think it's been so long since the star card has flipped on anybody?" Ami asked, pensive worry lining her face as if it had spelled out "worried" across her forehead. "Do you think the goddess thought we messed up with Marianna Black?"

"What's this 'we' stuff, compadre?" I joked. "I'm the one that got stuck with the taskmaster owl."

A deeper frown. "Well, since we can hear Archie, too, I just...I mean, I felt like this was about more than you, Astra. I mean, I'm the one with the cards, right?" Ami looked even more uneasy, her voice unsure. I glanced over and saw her blink back tears.

Great.

I hadn't even had my coffee, and I was the mean older sister already. The age difference between us sometimes seemed a vast, cavernous divide with a ledge I kept jumping off without thinking.

"Hey, hold on a second." I put the lip gloss down and turned to look at my three sisters one by one. "I was just making a joke. You three know I couldn't have found Marianna Black without your help, right? Ami, you're right—your cards pointed us to what we needed to do. Ayla, your ability to talk to ghosts was instrumental in finding the location. And Althea, without your concoction, Marianna could have died." The three of them beamed as I had never seen them shine, and they looked years younger. "Whatever reason I got stuck with this—"

"Stuck with this?" Ami asked breathlessly, her demeanor upbeat again. "Astra, I will never understand why you don't look at this as the honor that it is. The goddess Athena—"

"Okay, back off evangelist priestesses," I warned. "You know how I feel about the religious aspect, so let's not—"

"Hey, just one priestess," Ayla argued, crossing her arms. "I didn't say a thing. Don't lump me in with her!"

Mercifully, Aunt Gwennie called from downstairs to tell us the pancakes were getting cold, and we needed to hop to it.

MY MOTHER BEGAN breakfast with the "morning greeting" to her goddess (that we all had to sit through) and a five-minute silent meditation to greet the day. After her flowery speech, my three sisters and aunt quickly bowed their heads and closed their eyes—leaving me to eye the cooling pancakes unhappily as my stomach grumbled.

It wasn't easy being the only atheist witch in my mother's orbit, especially when my mother's orbit circled around devotion to the goddess Athena. A goddess, by the way, everyone at this table believed sent me a talking owl, some star power I didn't really know what to do with (or how it worked), and an assignment to stop impending murders when called upon to do so. It was kind of like the movie *Minority Report* crossed with Disney's *The Sword in the Stone*.

Actually, it wasn't really like that.

I'd left home at eighteen years old, joined the paranormal military, and did my level best to ignore my pious witch family and their devotion to a goddess I didn't believe existed. They did their level best to ignore my complete lack of belief and my choice to make a career out of something they disagreed with.

Actually, come to think of it…I didn't know what my sisters believed. I mean, really believed. All children give lip service to their parents' religion. That doesn't mean that deep down, they truly believed in anything.

I glanced at my sisters, eyes closed and mouths moving in silent devotion. Ami was five when I left; Althea, just an infant. Ayla was born while I was in the military, so until I moved home? I'd barely known her.

"Now, everyone, let's share what we thought about during our morning meditation," my mother, the chosen high priestess of the goddess Athena (so she said) on the planet Earth, said in soft tones. Her eyes glanced around the table and landed on me. "Astra, perhaps you wish to start this morning."

I sighed. "I just thought about the pancakes getting cold, Mom," I responded with a shrug. "You know I don't meditate. I haven't started meditating. I won't start meditating. Every time we stop to meditate at the breakfast table, I'm always going to be thinking about how hungry I am and that the food's getting cold." I reached out and took a sip of orange juice. "Anyone else?"

Mom frowned, and Aunt Gwennie sighed.

"You do that on purpose," Althea chided me.

The girl was half my age, and when she spoke, I would swear she was twice as old as me. "I think you practice those little speeches just to rile Mom up."

"She asks me on purpose, so yup." I smiled. "I don't meditate. I exercise."

"Nothing wrong with that. Astra, since you're so into the exercising thing? Why don't you sign up to run in the Forkbridge marathon," my Aunt Gwennie jumped in—no doubt to change the subject before my practices became the topic of the morning. She picked up a plate of eggs and passed it to Althea. "Alice Windrow is a customer of Ami's, and she's sponsoring the marathon to raise money for Fearless Fighters. It's a veterans organization for injured soldiers." My aunt looked over her nose at me. "That seems like it would be right up your alley."

"I've never run a marathon before." I watched the plate make its way slowly around the table. Too slowly.

"How hard can it be? You just, like, run until they tell you to stop, right?" Ayla asked. She snatched the plate of bacon from Althea and slid half of the slices onto her plate. "This is okay, right? Most of this is for me?"

"You're going to give yourself a heart attack," my mother told her.

"Yeah, but not for years, right?" Ayla said, her mouth full of bacon.

"A marathon is a bit harder than just running until you stop," I told Ayla as she chewed blissfully. "You have to start training for a marathon months before it takes place because it's a test of endurance." I turned to Aunt Gwennie. "When is it?"

"Is that true? I didn't know." My aunt frowned. "I believe it's just a few weeks away. I suppose that's not enough time, then?"

"I could do it," Ayla announced emphatically. "It's just running, right? That doesn't sound so hard."

"It doesn't, does it?" I asked, my eyebrow raised.

"Nope. I run all the time for fun. I could do it, no problem."

"Well," I told her, smiling. "I'd need more time to prepare and train, unfortunately."

Ayla looked at me with a cocky eyebrow raised. "I guess I'm better than you, then?"

When I first got here, my youngest sister was intimidated by me.

Apparently, those days were over.

"I'll tell you what. Tomorrow morning, you get up early. You and I will go for a run. If you can make it three miles without stopping? You can have the moonstone earrings I got from Imperatorial City that you drool over every time you come to my room."

Ayla's mouth dropped open—which was disgusting, considering it was filled with half-chewed bacon. "You're kidding me," she said, sounding like she had marbles in her mouth. "Don't you tease me, Astra! You know how much I like those earrings!"

"Ayla, don't talk with your mouth full," my mother scolded her.

"And you know how much those earrings cost me," I responded. "No, I'm not kidding. But you have to get up early in the morning, and I will try and wake you up once. Not twice, not three times —just once. If you don't get up, you forfeit the earrings."

Ayla chewed fast and swallowed loudly. Then she shouted, "You really mean it?"

I stood up and spat in my hand. Holding it across the table, I stared into my sister's eyes. "I oath that if you run three miles tomorrow without stopping, I will give you those earrings upon our return to the house. On my honor as a soldier."

She eyed me warily. "You're not a soldier anymore."

Ouch. "On my honor as a witch, then."

That seemed to satisfy her, and Ayla stood up quickly. I winced as she spit tiny pieces of bacon into her hand and shook mine emphatically. "Deal!"

"You're never going to get those earrings, little sister," Althea murmured with a half smile. She and Ami shared a glance and a chuckle.

Ayla's nostrils flared. "Oh, yeah? You just watch me!"

MY PHONE BUZZED while I was helping Aunt Gwennie with the breakfast dishes. We had no problem using magic to accomplish things, but apparently, someone decided a dishwasher was out of the question. "Where r u?"

"Finishing breakfast," I texted back.

"Hurry…reporter here soon."

I slipped my phone back into my utility belt.

"Is that Emma?" Aunt Gwennie asked me, handing me a freshly washed plate. I nodded as I took it and dried it with the dishtowel. "You two did an amazing job closing all of those cold cases. My friend Gertrude was ecstatic to get her lawn frog back after so many years."

Detective Emma Sullivan and I met a few weeks after I returned to Forkbridge, Florida. Our worlds rapidly collided when she was assigned to find the missing Marianna Black, and I was assigned (by the "goddess") to stop her murder.

Through the case, we became friends—helped, no doubt, by the fact that her brother was a vampire and had shared information about the paranormal world with her. That I was a witch and could get images from objects didn't faze her. In fact, she utilized my gifts better than the Ministry had.

"Some reporter from the *Forkbridge Gazette* wants to do a puff piece on us." I rolled my eyes. "I tried to beg off, and she didn't want to do it, either. I think her boss is making her do it. I don't want to leave her to deal with that on her own."

"You're a good friend, Astra," Aunt Gwennie said warmly. "I do wish the two of you would do more social things. Go out to a movie, maybe head into Orlando and go to one of the amusement parks. See a show. You know, have some fun." She scrubbed the skillet. "You two work too much."

"I like work."

Aunt Gwennie was still in her nightgown, her hair up in curlers. She gave me a warm smile, barely able to see me through her fogged-up glasses. "I know you like work, Astra, but that's not all there is."

"That sounds ridiculous coming from you, Aunt Gwennie. You and mom never do anything but priestess stuff and shop stuff and taking care of kids stuff." I put away the rest of the food into Tupperware and stored the leftovers in the fridge. There was, of course, no bacon left over. "When is the last time you went out to a movie or an amusement park? Or on a date?"

Aunt Gwennie looked surprised, and then she laughed uproariously. "Oh, Astra, darling, my dating days are long behind me. I'll be sixty before long. Sixty-year-old women don't date, dear."

"Sixty-year-old women date all the time, Aunt Gwennie. You're ridiculous."

"Astra, it's your turn now. You and your sisters. Your mother and I are quite happy with our lives the way they are. Simple, in devotion to the goddess and to you girls." She pulled off her glasses, cleaned them, and placed them delicately back on her nose. "You don't worry about me, dear. You worry about finding someone for you."

"I like my life pretty simple, too, Aunt Gwennie. I'm good." The last thing I needed was a romantic complication.

"Besides, she's got me, and I'm a handful," Archie, the owl, called in loudly through the open kitchen window. "I'm the goddess's own owl. I demand a lot of attention, you know," he informed us matter-of-factly. Then he burped.

"Excuse you, Archie," Aunt Gwennie said.

"Yeah, yeah, whatever," Archie retorted. "By the way, don't tell Ami I ate a rabbit."

"I hope you didn't eat the one she likes," Aunt Gwennie warned him.

"I hope she's smart enough not to get attached to the slow ones," he responded.

CHAPTER TWO

I drove to the station hoping for an uneventful day and a good interview.

"Hey, Astra." I closed my Jeep door and turned to find Officer Adam Granger watching me. The mid-twenties fresh-faced patrolman observed me with unblinking attention—as if waiting to catch me committing a crime. I wondered briefly if he practiced that expression in front of a mirror. "Beautiful morning, isn't it?" The stern stare melted into a smile, followed by a contented look once I nodded in agreement.

"Morning, Adam," I called back. I had no dispute with his observation. It was a bright early summer Florida morning. The seagulls circled above us, scouring for the day's dropped treats.

The air was crisp. It always amazed me that—despite the town not being right on the coast—I always caught the subtle scent of saltwater in the breeze. "It is a beautiful morning, as usual."

"So what? Probably means the afternoon storms will be even worse," a gruff voice complained from behind Granger. "The prettier the morning, the worse the afternoon. That's what I always say. It never fails. You watch. I don't have to be psychic to know that."

"And a good morning to you, Briggs!" I called to Granger's as yet unseen patrol partner. I'd spent enough time at the police department to know Vince Briggs's voice—and generally negative outlook—without needing to lay eyes on his stocky frame. "Not a weather witch, so I couldn't tell you yay or nay on the storms, but since it's June in Florida? I'm going to say you're likely more right than wrong, buddy."

Briggs popped out from behind the patrol car, his gray beard and hair clearly indicating his long service to the department. That he was still a patrolman out on the beat with that gray hair meant his attitude had gotten in his career's way much more often than not.

"Yes, well, good for you, girl," he barked. "What do you want, a medal?"

It hadn't taken me long to become friendly with most of the police department. Those who weren't friendly when I showed up became friendlier as Emma and I rapidly closed cold case after cold case. A few times we knocked an entire year's worth of cold cases out in a single day.

At least, the cold cases with items stored in the evidence locker that I could get information from.

Thanks to our partnership, Emma's star rose rapidly. Which, again, wasn't that hard in a small-town police department with only three other detectives and thirty officers. The three other detectives, incidentally, took retirement a mere two weeks after my arrival.

"I ain't gonna wind up working for no girl," one complained as he walked out the door. "It's enough that everybody makes fun of that ghost-talking camp. Now we got a psychic on the payroll, too. It ain't right." Someone told me he left the police station after his snit fit and made a beeline to the golf course to toast retirement with the other two.

Not surprising.

The mayor and the police chief, marveling at the solved case statistics, disagreed with Gruffy McGolfpants. They didn't care how Emma and I were doing it. They only cared it was finally, at long last, getting done—and getting done for a fraction of the cost of the initial investigations. The cherry on top? The three detectives leaving freed up enough money for Emma to get a raise and for me to be formally paid as a police consultant.

An impressive month, I'd say.

"Is today the day the reporter's coming to visit?" Adam asked.

Before I could answer, my phone vibrated again. "Yep. That's probably Emma griping at me for not being here yet." I smiled at the too-young-for-me officer and eyed him up and down. Adam was handsome, but he had the air of a man that cared little about that. I made a mental note to introduce him to Ami. "I need to go. You guys have a good day, and stay safe."

"Stay dry, you mean, when those storms roll in," Briggs grumbled.

Just then, Adam's radio crackled, reporting a complaint of an owl in someone's backyard.

Chasing rabbits.

MOST POLICE STATIONS were bustling with activity, but not Forkbridge. The chairs were empty, and the place was relatively quiet. I pushed my code into the electronic lock next to the reception window. Cassie Blackwood looked up and smiled at me after I buzzed in.

"Even when you're going to be interviewed by the newspaper, you're still going to wear that diving outfit, are you?" The old woman was a fixture at the reception desk. At sixty-six, she'd been here longer than any police officer, and I was sure she knew twice as much as any of them. "Someday, we are going to have to get you into regular clothes."

"I like my clothes, Cassie. Besides, it's a newspaper article. They don't care what I look like."

She laughed, and it was like the sound of sandpapered bells. "She brought a photographer, dear. If I know Meryl Hawkins, you and Emma are going to be on the front page above the fold." Looking back down at her papers, she pointed toward a hallway without looking. "You better get going. The chief wants this article to be flattering, and it won't do anyone good if she has to write that you were late."

"I'm not late," I mumbled, but I sped up my steps anyway.

"There she is!" Chief Daniel Harmon called across the room. With his back against the wall, hands at his sides, the chief looked rigidly alert. The chief always looked rigidly alert, though. "Astra, please, join us. I don't believe you've met Meryl Hawkins. Ms. Hawkins, this is our official police psychic, Astra Arden."

I extended my gloved hand. "Pleased to meet you, Ms. Hawkins."

The reporter stared transfixed at my hand—but refused to shake. Finally, she glanced up at me and met my eyes. "Is there a reason for the gloves, Ms. Arden?"

"You don't want her poking around in your head, do you?" Emma quipped as she walked out of the break room holding two cups of coffee. "Nice of you to join us, Arden. No psychic connection to a clock, I guess?" She handed one cup to the chief.

I glanced at the clock on the wall. I was a mere five minutes late.

Just five minutes.

Emma Sullivan never met a ball she didn't want to bust.

"I don't poke around in people's heads. That's

not a particular talent I have." Within three words of my speaking, I heard the distinct click of a tape recorder turning on. Behind Meryl, a skinny young man crept between us with his camera and snapped a close-up picture of my nostrils. "I can read the histories of objects and, sometimes, people. But I don't do it unless it's necessary."

"Could you read this pen?" Meryl asked, tilting the pen toward me.

"I could, but what I do isn't a parlor trick," I told her somewhat defensively.

The chief frowned, and Emma froze. Her eyes widened to the size of half dollars, then she swallowed. Glaring at me as if to remind me her future career depended on this interview going well, she turned toward the reporter.

Pasting a gigantic, friendly (and out of character) smile on her face, Emma said, "What Astra means is she only utilizes her talent for specific purposes. She doesn't just go around randomly grabbing things and sifting through the mental images she gets." The detective jerked her chin toward my still-outstretched hand. "That's the reason for the gloves. They keep her from getting any images unless she's intending on reading an object."

"It also keeps her from getting too tired,"

Chief Harmon added. "I imagine it's a muscle like anything else, and too much use can exhaust her. I came into the station many a day," he added proudly, "to see these two in the conference room, Astra hard at work uncovering information we never would've gotten any other way. She looked like she'd been up all night and on into the morning."

"Well, obviously, we're all very impressed with Forkbridge PD's ability to close so many older cases. But I have to ask—are we sure this woman's information is correct?" Meryl pointed at me without looking at me. "Wouldn't it be an absolute tragedy if we found out this is nothing more than psychic hokum, and men and women were put in jail based on the say-so of a charlatan?" Meryl blinked innocently, her pen poised on her pad.

I did my best to keep my face deadpan, because I knew that was the way to take what she said, but whatever emotion I kept my face from betraying? Emma...did not.

Her face reddened with vexation, she stepped closer to the reporter and leaned in. "I'm a military veteran, and a trained police officer, Ms. Hawkins," Emma told the reporter, meeting her eyes boldly. "This may be a small town, and many of these crimes may be small crimes, but they were important to the people they happened to. Astra is one tool of many tools that we use to get information. Like any decent police officer that knows the law, I confirm or discard that information after thorough traditional investigation—"

"Oh, of course. I never meant to imply otherwise." The reporter interrupted Emma's head of steam and waved away her previous statements. "Though now that you mention it— did you have to discard much of her information?" Meryl Hawkins asked coldly. "How much? What percentage would you say? After all, I think the taxpayers would like to know what percentage of this woman's salary is wasted on bogus information that our fine police officers have to spend time chasing down." The woman smiled like a snake. "Don't you?"

A flashbulb popped, and the chief threw a dark glance at me.

I grabbed the top of my full-length glove and yanked it down before anyone could speak. Meryl Hawkins opened her mouth to say something, but I snatched the pen from her hand before she could start whatever new thought was in her head about my uselessness. "Are you sure?" I asked, holding the pen up in my bare hand.

"Please," she answered with a viper's grin.

I closed my eyes. Images flashed through my mind. A man with dark hair signing a check for twenty thousand dollars. A letter being written to Meryl apologizing for leaving and going back to his family. A request never to speak of their affair, that it would ruin his political career. That he hoped paying for college would make up for the pain he caused. My eyes popped open. "Do you really want me to talk about the twenty thousand dollars?"

Meryl Hawkins' face paled slightly beneath her copious amounts of makeup, and she shifted from foot to foot. Her mouth opened, then closed.

For a second, I gloated to witness her sudden and intense discomfort, but I realized that glee made me a bit too much like her.

"I, um, I'm not sure what you're talking about," she said.

Yes, you are. Your face is telling everyone you are. "A check that you got, along with a letter, from—"

"Yes, well, I don't know that what you're seeing is entirely accurate." Meryl snatched the pen from my hand, being remarkably careful not to touch me. "But you've said enough that I can see clearly you have the capability you claim you have. Even if what you see isn't the whole truth. Obviously." I watched the expensive pen disappear into her purse.

Chief Harmon held out a cheap ballpoint pen politely. "Please, take mine."

"I don't think I need one, thank you," Meryl told him. "We've got all we need for the story." She cleared her throat. "I think I'll leave any investigative exposés for the future. After all, Astra has only been here one month, and closing all of those cold cases is definitely a milestone that should be celebrated without complications." She looked at me pointedly. "Perhaps we should leave any unpleasantness unsaid at this point."

I stared back and said nothing.

"Well, Ms. Hawkins, the Forkbridge Police Department would certainly appreciate some good press for a change," Chief Harmon told the reporter with noticeable relief. "You're more than welcome to get any information you need or to continue the interview in the conference room if you—"

"No, no, I think that'll be all. We've got several interviews scheduled with some of the people you've helped, and I think that should be the focus." She leaned over and grabbed her bag. "The Gundersons are just ecstatic you helped find the terrible people that stole their labradoodle. Everyone likes a dog story." She smiled briefly at each one of us. "If I need anything, I'll let you know."

"Please do that," Chief Harmon told her. "Let me walk you out."

"I FEEL like I could've stayed home," I told Emma. We watched the three make their way toward the front door, the photographer skulking along behind like an inept bodyguard. Emma pointed toward several bottles of pink liquid on her desk, and I shook my head. "Not thirsty, thanks. And not sure I'd drink a sports drink that bright pink color. Anyway, did she get any information from you at all, or was that just the shortest interview in the history of interviews?"

"I think she planned to do some pseudo-exposé on the evils of psychics. Which, to be honest, has nothing to do with psychics. She dated some guy from the Cassandra spiritualist camp years ago, and he left her to go live on an ashram in India." Emma sat down at her desk and rolled her eyes. "I don't think she ever got over it."

"Well, then she's got terrible taste in men."

Emma stared at me curiously. "Really now? What did you see with that pen that got her so freaked out?"

"Let's just say she had an affair with a married politician as a young woman," I told Emma, my voice low. "When he went back to his wife, it appears he bought her a journalism degree as a parting gift."

Emma stared at me, shocked. "Wow, are you kidding?"

"Not kidding. The images were super clear."

"Did you recognize the politician?"

I nodded. "Not going to tell you who it is."

Emma looked disappointed, but she eventually nodded. "I get it. But still. You're a spoilsport. What good is it having a psychic as a friend when I can't find out all the juicy bits everybody hides?"

"The good is that you close a whole bunch of cold cases, everyone sings your praises for finding a psychic that can help you do that, and you run off the other three lazy, misogynistic detectives that can't stand the idea of you being super-detective with the highest close rate in the state of Florida overnight."

Emma sighed. "Yeah, well, there is that."

It was the Forkbridge mayor in the images from the reporter's pen.

Since the mayor was so enthusiastic about my coming on to the Forkbridge Police Department, I suspected Meryl Hawkins's desire to make me look bad had as much to do with him as her hatred of all things psychic because of the ashram dude.

"The important thing is she knows I know who he is," I told Emma as I sat down across from her. "I don't think we'll have any problem with the *Forkbridge Gazette*. At least not for a while."

"That's good." Emma tilted her head and raised her eyebrow. "It's that obnoxious house representative, isn't it? The one that's always on *Fox News* yammering about immigrants and white people?"

"Not going to tell you."

"Spoilsport."

CHAPTER THREE

The following day I stood in Ayla's bedroom doorway at half-past five, ready for our brisk three-mile morning run. (Or, to be more accurate, however many miles of a run I would get to have before my younger sister gave up.) Her bedroom was dark, the curtains drawn, and a soft snore emerged from somewhere within the pile of blankets.

I cleared my throat. "Ayla."

She didn't move or open her eyes.

"Ayla, it's time," I said, a little louder.

Nothing. Not a movement, not a sound.

I crossed my arms and leaned against the door frame. "Ayla!"

Her eyes popped open in surprise, and she

looked solidly about. Finally, she found me in the doorway and regarded me blearily without lifting her head from her pillow. My youngest sister groaned. "What?" she glanced sleepily at the clock. "It's not even six. Go back to bed."

"I said I was going to wake you up early."

"This isn't early. This is the middle of the night!" Ayla complained. "Everyone is still asleep! Everyone should be asleep. I should be asleep. Go away!"

"That's not true. I'm not asleep. I'm dressed and ready to go." I waited for her response, but got only a glare. "Come on, sleepyhead, do you want those earrings or not?"

Her eyes swept up and down, and then she closed them. "I don't want anything this early in the morning," Ayla mumbled. "Go away." She pulled her blanket over her head and burrowed back into her pillow like a bear returning to hibernation after discovering it was the dead of winter. "Come back in two hours. We can go do the running thing then. Two hours. Thanks."

I sighed a little too loudly. A little too dramatically. Then I clapped my hands together just loud enough to be sure the sound would annoy her. "Well, I guess this settles the argument about which one of us is better, doesn't it? Enjoy the rest of your sleep, Ayla. I'm going out for my morning run." I grabbed the door loudly and made sure the creaking went well and long as I closed the door. "Night, lazybones."

Ayla popped straight up, her disheveled hair sticking up in every direction. Clutching her coverlet to her chest, she glared at me. "Just because someone doesn't want to go running at the butt crack of dawn doesn't make them a worse runner."

"It does make them late to a marathon," I pointed out. "When do you think those things usually start, anyway? After shopping and brunch?"

"Not this early!"

"Sometimes, it's even earlier. Yes, sometimes it's slightly later. But the one you're running today?" I gestured toward the clock. "It starts in five minutes, with or without you." I gave her a pointed look. "I invited you to join me, remember?"

"So?"

"So you go when I go. This is Florida. It's hot and humid, and it's easy to get dehydrated if we run too late in the day. Right now, the sun's just barely coming up. It's the best time of the day to run." She stared at me with glassy, resentful eyes.

"Look, I've extended the invitation, and I told you I was going to try and wake you up just once." I held out my hand. "This was that attempt. From here, you make your own decision."

"What does that mean?"

"It means I'm going on my run in five minutes. Whether you're there or not."

I WAS STILL STRETCHING along the back porch railing when Ayla stomped out. Her disheveled hair was pulled back into a messy ponytail, and she was dressed in a heavy tracksuit that would, within minutes, likely cause her to overheat. "Don't you have a pair of shorts and a tank top?" I asked her.

"You're not wearing one. It's chilly," Ayla complained sullenly. "If I wear shorts and a tank top, I'm going to be cold."

"If you wear that, within a few minutes, you're going to be really hot."

"Quit ordering me around! I know what I'm doing!"

Oh, boy.

She didn't, but I would not argue with her.

Her expression told me she was stuck in a teenager's snit and not likely to listen to reason.

"Have you stretched?" I asked her.

"I'm ready whenever you are," she answered without answering.

I paused for a second and considered her. On the one hand, I was doing this to teach her a lesson. Not a mean lesson, mind you. Ayla's overconfidence was something she would need to learn to rein in before it got her into trouble. I knew this from experience. I also knew she wouldn't be able to run three miles consistently. I'd seen her get winded running a half block.

But I didn't want her injured. If she didn't warm up her muscles before starting, there was a chance that could happen.

"What are you waiting for?" she snapped at me, glaring.

Then again, maybe a pulled groin muscle would cause her to think twice before bragging mastery of something she'd never done before. "Nothing at all. Let's go."

I started with a slow jog toward the driveway and winced as Ayla's feet pounded the cement hard and fast in an attempt to overtake me. "Ayla," I said over my shoulder. "This isn't a race. We're going running together. Slow down"

"I can totally beat you!" she told me enthusiastically as she passed me on the driveway. Her thundering, stomping steps made me wince for the joint pain she would feel when she was my mother's age if she kept running like that. "Bet you can't catch me!"

"Ayla, you know the saying 'this is a marathon, not a sprint'?" I asked, keeping my steady pace. "Marathons require slow, steady, relentless pacing." She kept running like a bat out of hell toward the street, and I gently accelerated my own pace to catch up with her. "If you're trying to sprint, you can explode your speed, try and go as fast as you can, but a marathon? You want to keep a gentle, steady pace—Ayla!"

Ayla's frenetic, bouncy steps brought her to the road faster than I'd anticipated, and she'd careened into it without looking. The sedan drove at a reasonable speed toward the main street, but Ayla still nearly ran dead in front of it.

My shout got her attention, and she stopped at the last minute, scrambling to back up as the car's brakes screeched. The momentum propelled her forward, sliding on the gravel, and she nearly toppled over—stopped only by another runner coming in the opposite direction at just the right time to grab her.

"Are you all right?" I heard him ask as he pulled her toward the curb, her back to the car that almost hit her.

Ayla looked more shaken than I'd ever seen her, and she stared at the man as if bewildered by the turn of events. Behind her, a businessman jumped out of the stopped car. The poor man looked horrified. "I am so sorry, she just came out of nowhere! Honey, are you okay?" The businessman reached Ayla the same time I did, both of us looking to the jogger—who was politely but expertly examining Ayla for injuries.

"I don't think she hit anything; she's just gotten the daylights scared out of her, that's all," the man told us both. He turned to me. "I take it she's yours?"

"My sister," I answered, nodding.

"I am so terribly sorry," the businessman repeated. "I have kids of my own about her age, and...I'm just so sorry. I'm sorry I didn't see her sooner. Are you sure she didn't bump into the car? I didn't hear any clunks but—"

"I didn't hit anything," Ayla whispered, her cheeks pink with embarrassment. Her chin was down, and her eyes glued to the black asphalt. "I'm sorry. I was showing off for my sister, and I wasn't looking where I was going." She raised her eyes up and looked at the driver. "I'm really sorry, mister."

As annoyed as I was at her behavior, Ayla's reaction reminded me how young she was. I tamped down the desire to explode at her for her reckless behavior. "The important thing is that nobody's hurt," I said (sounding remarkably like my Aunt Gwennie).

The driver and I exchanged information in case it was needed, but I assured him I didn't think it would be. He reluctantly returned to his car and drove to work—most likely hoping his day would get better.

"You two training for the Forkbridge marathon?" the runner (who'd saved my sister from being smashed into a pancake by an Oldsmobile) asked with a smile. He looked kindly at Ayla as if attempting to disarm her embarrassment and soothe her nerves with charm.

"Yes. Okay, no. I've never run before," my sister admitted, her cheeks turning pink again. "I mean, I've run like across the backyard and stuff. I thought I could run three miles easy." Ayla looked apprehensively at me. "My sister didn't think I could do it. And maybe she was right. I didn't even get out of the driveway."

"Well, you got out of the driveway," he laughed. "That was part of the problem. You ran out of it just a little too fast." Ayla's cheeks went from pink to red, and she shifted uncomfortably from foot to foot. The man crouched down and looked up at her. "I am training for the marathon, but it took me a while to work up to it. Most people start smaller, like a 5K. Then a 10K. Then, maybe, a half marathon. A full marathon is a pretty big deal, and they're not easy. You got off your couch, though, so you're already in the game."

Ayla raised her eyebrow. "But aren't there long and short marathons?"

"A marathon is 26.2 miles, Ayla," I told her.

The man looked up at me. "You run?"

"I run, but I've never done a marathon." Unless you count listening to my mother's lecture on what I should do with my life as a marathon. In that case, I have. Many of them. "I just run for exercise, to clear my head."

He nodded and stood up. "Jason Bishop," he said, extending his hand.

I reached forward with my gloved hand. "Astra Arden. This is my sister, Ayla."

"Nice to meet you both."

Jason was tall, with a slender runner's frame,

and dressed in a tight tank top and shorts. His brown hair had sun-bleached highlights I was sure were natural, and his clean-shaven face had a boyish charm to it—even though I was pretty sure he was close to my age. "I run this route every morning, but no one else does, so it's usually pretty solitary. To tell you the truth, I wouldn't mind some company," he said with a friendly smile. "Shall we?" Before we even agreed, he was moving his limbs to warm his muscles.

Ayla looked at me, her face nervous and her eyes frightened. "Do you still want to even go?" There was a short pause. "I mean, with me?"

"Of course I do. I wasn't the one that was almost hit by a car, though. Do you feel up to it?"

My sister stared back at me, her expression torn.

Jason stopped stretching and put his hands on his hips. "I could totally understand you not wanting to go today, considering what happened. Only the toughest of the tough could get up after that near-catastrophe and just do what they intended to do as if nothing happened," Jason told Ayla, his eyes twinkling. "Those people? They are super rare. One in a million. Hardly ever find them." He stretched his arms wide as if he were a windmill. "Most people don't bounce back so easily, so don't feel like you have to—"

"I'll do it!" Ayla chirped and flapped her arms to mimic Jason's graceful sweeping motions. "I just have to warm up first!"

Oh. Right.

Now she has to warm up.

"Hey, hey, you want to do it a little slower than that," he said as he stepped forward to help. Before he laid hands on my thirteen-year-old sister, he looked over at me with a questioning look as if silently asking for permission.

I was impressed and nodded.

Then he turned to her, stepped slightly closer, and asked, "May I?"

Ayla thought for a moment and then nodded.

MY SISTER MADE it half a mile from the house before she gave up.

And to be honest?

I think that was a quarter-mile further than she would've made it had the handsome Jason Bishop not been coaching her the whole way.

"It hurts so much!" Ayla wheezed as we walked halfway up the driveway. "My thighs feel like they are on fire! My feet are so hot! Everything is all sweaty, and it feels so gross! Why does anybody do this!"

"It'll get better," Jason told her. "It's hard at first, and it doesn't seem like it feels good, but trust me, Ayla, if you keep at it? Eventually, it feels great. And it's good for your health— mentally, physically. I hope you stick with it."

"I think you're a massive liar," she told him, her face glum. Then she whirled on her heel and sauntered up the driveway toward the house, muttering to herself.

"For her first time, she did great," Jason told me once Ayla was out of earshot. "It's hard to keep up a good attitude when your leg muscles are on fire."

"You're really good with kids," I told him. "This is the first day I tried to get her to run, and I couldn't get her to stretch or drink water or not sprint. But you? You're a natural." He smiled appreciatively. "You must have kids."

"Twenty-seven of them, in fact," he laughed.

I was not shockable, but I have to admit that statement shocked me. Jason laughed at my expression, and I raised my eyebrow. "Just how much of a player were you after high school, Mr. Bishop?"

"I'm a teacher at Forkbridge Junior High," Jason said, gesturing toward the center of town. "No kids of my own, but I get a new batch every single year, and every single year one of them forces me to up my game. Just when I think I have it all figured out, I get that one kid that's decided they're going to be the one to trip me up."

I smiled. "And do they?"

"Only a few times." He shrugged with charming nonchalance. "Like I said, each new class comes with new lessons."

Jason and I stretched as we spoke, cooling down as the sun rose full in the eastern sky. He looked up, and suddenly, he was startled. "Wow, is that an owl?" Squinting toward the top of the trees, he pointed. "You see it?" Yeah, I saw it. "That's just crazy. It's just staring at us."

"Is it now?" I asked distractedly. "Interesting." I made a mental note to myself to talk with Archie. That bird needed to give me some privacy when…Nope, scratch that. Just needed to give me some privacy.

Jason marveled at Archie's steady focus on the two of us for a few more minutes and then stood up. "Well, I need to get home and get a shower. School starts early for teachers. If the kids had any idea how early, it might make them stop complaining about their own schedules." I nodded. He paused for a moment as if thinking about something and then said, "Since I'm training for the marathon, I'm running every morning now." I nodded again. He smiled. "Same time tomorrow?"

I hadn't intended to run every day, but suddenly, that didn't sound like a bad idea. "Sure, same time tomorrow. Do you want me to leave Ayla home? She might slow you down, especially since you're training—"

"Not at all! I'll make sure to do the lion's share of my intense running before I meet up with the two of you. I can use the last bit of running as a cool down." I nodded. Jason stuck his hand out again to shake. "It was very nice to meet you, Astra."

"You, too, Jason," I responded (without a nod this time) and shook his hand. "And thanks again for keeping my sister from becoming a large, overconfident stain on the asphalt. I'm not sure how I would've explained that to my mother."

"I'm sure her overconfidence stems from seeing her older sister as a representation of the incredible woman she has the possibility of becoming," he told me just before he turned around and ran off gracefully.

I stared after him, my mind blank as I absorbed his last comment.

"That sounded like flirting to me!" Archie yelled down from the top of the tree.

"Oh, shut up," I muttered, too low for the owl to hear, and went inside.

BY THE AFTERNOON, you would think Ayla had spent the morning being tortured by medieval elves that suspected she stole one of their treasures.

"I don't want to move," Ayla moaned. She lay on the couch in the great room, her feet up on the armrest, moaning, and whining. "Everything hurts. Everything. Why does anybody do this? No one should do this."

"You think it hurts now?" I called from the herb room (where I was doing Ayla's stocking chore). "Wait until you wake up tomorrow. The worst soreness is always the morning after. Make sure you eat bananas today. The potassium will help. Maybe Althea has something better. We'll have to ask her after her shop shift."

"This gets worse?" she asked, her voice panicked. I didn't answer, focusing instead on neatly stacking the frankincense in the storage room, so Aunt Gwennie didn't complain. After a few silent minutes—punctuated every so often by moaning—Ayla called, "Is Jason going to come tomorrow if we go?"

"He said he'd swing by at the end of his run if we'd like to do the last few miles with him." I closed the stocked cabinet and opened the empty one below. "The best thing for you as a runner is to get used to running every day if you can. Eventually, not much soreness at all. If you skip a day or a few, though, it's harder to start up again."

"He was super cute," my younger sister said.

"Uh-huh," I answered noncommittally.

"How could you not think he's cute?"

"I didn't say I didn't think he was cute."

Suddenly, a door slammed. "Astra! Astra, where are you?" Ami shouted, sounding panicked.

"I'm in the herb room putting away the frankincense that just came in," I shouted. "Are you okay?"

"I'm fine, but I was doing reading for Alice Windrow, and that card came up," she shouted as she skidded into the herb room. "You need to come quick!"

CHAPTER FOUR

"She's super into all the psychic stuff, so you can just tell her what's going on, and she'll totally get it," Ami said as we hurried into the shop. The tinkling of crystals from the dream catchers hanging from the ceiling and the heavy scent of lotus incense didn't touch Ami's visible anxiety. "I told her I was going to get you."

Alice Windrow stood near a small wishing fountain next to the cashier station. She held the glowing star card held gingerly between her thumb and forefinger as she scanned the shelves of candles. "There must be a candle in just this color," she told Aunt Gwennie. "I mean, if I'm special enough to get a card like this, there has to be a reason." Alice waived the card in the air. "Just look at how cute it is! All sparkly and golden!"

My aunt, her face pale, stood behind the smartly dressed woman. She glanced toward me, her eyes pleading. "What do I tell her?" she mouthed silently.

"Alice, this is my sister Astra," Ami said. "The card is glowing because Astra—" Ami's face twisted in frustration. "Well, maybe I should let her tell you."

"You didn't tell her anything?"

Ami shook her head no.

It's funny how we all were in this together whenever it wasn't super important, or there wasn't something hard to do. As soon as things got a little tricky, or it was time for someone to deliver bad news? This was all my thing.

"It's nice to meet you, Alice," I stepped around Ami and waited for the woman to turn. She didn't. "Alice?"

The distracted heiress plucked a small container of lucky oil off the shelf next to the candles. "Oh, I need this," she murmured cheerfully, continuing her shopping with reckless abandon—ignoring me and the turn her life was about to take. "I can't believe none of these candles match that glow, but the oil will work. It has that same golden hue to it."

"I think you're going to need more than lucky oil," I told her seriously.

Her eyes flitted from point to point, settling nowhere.

Aunt Gwennie stepped forward and took the oil from Alice. Then my aunt gently grabbed her arm and turned her to face me. "I'll keep this up at the register for you, but I think you need to talk to Astra. And Alice, please listen carefully to what she has to say." She frowned with a curious squint. "Promise me you'll pay attention, Alice. That card is a serious message."

"Oh, I only get serious messages when I come in here." Alice Windrow waved away my aunt's concern. "I always listen to what you girls have to say, you know that. Just because I don't let it get me down or make me depressed? It doesn't mean I don't listen to any of you."

"Did she just call you a girl?" I asked my aunt, my eyebrow raised. Alice looked to be about twenty-five years old, give or take, but she had an incredibly sunny demeanor that made her seem girlish.

"Did you just call me old?" my aunt murmured back.

Archie flew in from the backyard, his eyes wide. "I got a message that we got a job. Do we?" the owl asked. Jutting his wide-eyed face toward Alice, his big, expressive eyeballs swept her up and down. "Is she our job?"

"An owl!" Alice squealed, clapping her hands like a ten-year-old who had just seen elephants at the circus for the first time. "Did an owl just fly in here? Is the owl for me, too? How exciting!" She jumped up and down and clapped her hands—again—with joy.

Lowering my voice, I leaned toward Ami. "Is she for real?" I'd never met someone in their mid-twenties quite so squeally before. The childish exuberance would be adorable in someone much younger—and in a much different situation. It was jarring coming from a grown woman marked for death. "She on drugs or something?"

Ami glared at me. "Alice has been coming in here for readings since her parents died," she informed me with a hand on her hip. "She very much believes in the world of the unseen and follows the path of the pixies." Ami leaned forward. "Her demeanor is similar to those who follow the path of the pixies because—"

"I got it, I got it." Pixies were tiny elf-like creatures fond of dancing, singing, and general frolicking—usually outdoors. In folklore, pixies are known to be benign, mischievous, short, and very childlike. They bring blessings to those fond of them and "lessons" to those who are not.

In reality, pixies can be a real pain in the keister.

Sure, they can be kind and generous to people they like, but they can really trip up people they don't. If they like you, they may help you win the lottery and become wealthy beyond your wildest dreams. If they don't, or if you disappoint them somehow? They can "accidentally on purpose" make a piano fall on your head.

Alice Windrow was a pixie follower and marked for death?

That made this situation…complicated.

I scanned the room to make sure no pixies were hiding in any corners and explained the situation to fate's latest potential victim.

"Wow." Alice stared at me, her eyes as wide as saucers after I got done briefly explaining the situation. "So, you mean the goddess Athena herself doesn't want me to die? Like, the goddess

Athena who lives on Mount Olympus? That goddess Athena?"

I nodded. "It appears that way."

"And she's so sure I might die that she sent that card to warn me?" Alice pointed.

"Yes."

"But she doesn't tell you who wants to kill me, or why, or what you need to protect me from?" Alice's eyebrow raised. "You have to figure it all out yourself?"

"You've about summed it up."

I know what you're thinking. Did I believe that the goddess herself was doing all this now? After all, I just claimed that to Alice Windrow.

No, not yet.

What am I talking about, "not yet"?

No, I don't.

But I was finding it far easier just to go with the flow, to accept the explanations given to me —even if I didn't entirely believe them. Sometimes, you just have to go with the paranormal flow.

It's easier that way.

"I can't think of anyone that would want to kill me. I try to be nice to absolutely everyone! That's the pixie path, after all," Alice told me, nodding eagerly. "Well, that's not the entire pixie path, but I haven't punched anyone in a really long time."

I blinked. "I'm sorry, you punched someone as part of your religion?"

"Only when they deserved it. That's part of the pixie path, too, you know. Reward with love when met with love, reward with a sock in the nose when met with hate." I found the intensity of her brown eyes paired with her positive response both disconcerting and oddly amusing. "But like I said, I haven't had to punch anyone in a really long time."

I shook my head and turned toward Ami. "What were you giving Alice a reading on?"Ami opened her mouth to answer, but I added, "Can you think of where you were in the reading when the star card showed up?" Once more, my sister tried to respond. "Oh, and did it show up right at the beginning or in the middle?"

Ami stared at me, her arms crossed.

"I'm done."

"Are you sure?" she asked with exaggerated patience. I nodded. "I was giving her a Celtic Cross reading, and it came down when we got to external influences," Ami explained. She turned and walked over to her reading table. "Here, I can show you. The reading was about the marathon and how it was going to go. Alice wanted to know if there was anything she needed to be aware of that she wasn't."

"Someone wanting her dead certainly qualifies," Aunt Gwennie said, joining us around the reading table.

I glanced at the spread. The cards seemed relatively innocuous at first glance. Lots of cups, lots of wands, relatively few cards that denoted any problems. "How does the star card show up?" I asked Ami. "Do you flip the card over when you lay out the original reading, or does it come up some other way?"

"No, actually. Well, last time when I was doing Marianna Black's reading? It did. When I was laying out the cards for the reading, the star card flipped over already glowing." Ami pointed to the table. "That card originally in that spot? I could've sworn that card was the devil." The side door to the shop opened, and my mother walked in. "In fact, if I had to stake my life on it? I'd swear that was the card."

"And then what happened?" I asked.

"Alice and I started talking about the reading. A few minutes later, I looked down. The star card was there, and it was glowing." Ami looked perplexed. "I have no idea how it got there. I didn't see it happen. It was just suddenly…there."

"That's how I remember it, too," Alice nodded. "When I saw the devil card flipped over, I thought…well, I thought…" Her face turned bright red, and she looked away shyly. "I mean, we all know what that card sometimes means, right? So I thought maybe…" We stared at her with knowing looks. "Look, it's been a while, okay?"

For those who are unaware, the devil card can mean physical pleasures.

Let's just leave it at that.

"I get it, but that's not all it means," Ami told her. "You're pretty wealthy, and it can be about an overabundance of luxury or problems with business matters. I mean, it can mean a lot of things. Point to a lot of things. It doesn't have to mean a make-out session with some hot marathon runner."

Alice looked slightly disappointed.

"Was it reversed?" I asked Ami, hoping the card was in its more favorable position. My sister shook her head no. "Okay, since it wasn't reversed, we can assume the card was in its warning position with more negative connotations, and it was in the position of outside influences, so…ugh, okay. Archie," I called. "Are we still on the same timetable as last time?"

The owl, perched on the back of a chair watching us, flapped his wings slightly. "Seventy-two hours," he responded. "You got seventy-two hours to stop what's going to happen. It's not exact, though. It could be a little more, it could be a little less."

Despite Alice Windrow's typical (slightly infantile) giddiness, I could see she took the discussions and the situation seriously. She watched us while nervously chewing her lower lip. Finally, she asked quietly, "What do I do?"

"Well, the last time this happened, the person ran out screaming and got themselves kidnapped. So I would suggest you not take that route." I turned to Ami. "The last time this happened, we didn't have the cooperation of the person who was at risk, so this is a bit new."

A brief silence fell as we all contemplated what our next steps should be.

It was far more convenient to have Alice Windrow aware of the situation and seemingly willing to work with us than to be running along behind her trying to figure things out. But the lack of information any of us had, including

Alice, still made it frustrating to formulate a plan of attack.

"I'm really sorry, Alice," Ami, deeply apologetic, told her customer. "I mean, I'm glad that you came in for a reading, and we found out that something is going on, but…I don't know, I'm just really sorry."

Mom walked over and put her arm around Ami. "It's not your fault."

"I know. I just feel bad."

"You girls have been chosen for a great task by the goddess, and because Alice is a follower of the pixies, I'm sure they will be very grateful to you, too." Mom looked as if the pride would just burst out of her. "And you too, Alice. Not many people are chosen by the goddess Athena as worthy of being saved." My mother smiled benevolently. "We always knew you were a special person, but now you have confirmation."

I did my best not to roll my eyes.

"I'm going to call Emma Sullivan at the Forkbridge Police Department, with your permission, of course." Alice nodded vigorously. "I want to make her aware of the fact that a crime might be committed within the next three or four days."

"And then what?" Aunt Gwennie asked.

"And then Alice is going to answer some questions for us instead of the other way around," I told her. "Comfortable with that, Alice?"

"Whatever you guys need," she told me. Turning to Aunt Gwennie, she asked for the small bottle of lucky oil back. "I think I want the extra-large bottle instead, please."

I TALKED TO EMMA, giving her the rundown on the situation, then stepped out onto the back porch to wait. She assured me she'd be over within fifteen minutes—and I assured her we wouldn't start without her.

After a minute, Archie joined me.

"So, tell me truthfully—if this had something to do with the pixies marking her for death because she offended them, would you be aware of it?" I asked him.

I didn't want to insult Alice's religion in front of her, but I dealt with the pixies on numerous occasions. I'd had the unfortunate experience of chasing one that was a fugitive. Individual pixies were frustrating, but if you made an entire group of them mad?

Look out.

Archie clicked his beak, then said, "The pixies wouldn't mark someone for death."

I glared at him.

He stared back. "Fine. The pixies usually wouldn't mark a human for death."

I raised an eyebrow.

"Okay, when the Witches' Council was in charge, and the government would execute or imprison people for letting the humans know about the paranormal world, the pixies wouldn't break those rules. Most of the time," Archie said with a mocking bow. "Now that the paranormal government is all species-rights minded? I don't know. When people start setting up new rules, there are always groups that want to push the line. Are the pixies those people?" Archie shrugged his wings. "I don't know."

"So she could have done something to upset the pixies."

"Well, they're pixies. They are tactful, diplomatic, cordial, and affable—right up until the moment that they aren't." Archie waved his wing in the air. "You know we're going to have to talk to them if we want to rule them out."

"You're the goddess's own owl," I told him with faux respect. He rolled his eyes. "You'd probably get a lot farther than I would in getting an audience with them because of Athena. Can't you go talk to them? Come back and let me know what they said?"

He made a sour face. "I'm supposed to help you do this job. Not do this job for you."

I made a face back.

He clicked his beak at me.

I leaned against one of the porch supports and looked out over the backyard. I spotted a rabbit in the corner of the field, and felt Archie's sudden tense alertness. "Leave it alone. We've got bigger things to worry about. And if Ami comes out here and sees you, you'll be sleeping at Parrot Paradise."

He made a sound that sounded like a hiss.

"Seriously, though—the devil card, in that position?" I shifted nervously as I thought about that card. Yes, sure, no tarot cards were really "evil." The death card didn't mean death, and the lovers card didn't mean you were going to immediately find a partner. The cards meant different things in different positions. Experienced readers like Ami could interpret them to fashion a story the customer needed to hear. But that card in that position in this situation? "That's not good."

"Somebody is trying to exploit little Miss

Moneybucks," Archie said with a sigh. "That's what you're thinking, aren't you?"

"Well, if we have seventy-two hours, it could have something to do with the marathon, too." I turned and faced the bird. "The marathon is three days away, so the timing lines up. I don't think it has anything to do with the pixies, but I feel like we have to check." I frowned. "Also, I mean, she's a pixie follower—why aren't they protecting her?"

"Why do the pixies do anything?" Archie asked. "They're like children. Crazy, rambunctious, mischievous, drunk children. With a god complex."

"Right, like you're one to talk about anyone else having a god complex," I snorted.

Just then, the back door opened, and Alice Windrow came out. "I'm sorry to interrupt. Ami explained that you and the owl can talk to each other, so I figure you're discussing the situation. My situation." The girlish lilt to her voice was gone, replaced by a guileless and trusting tone. "I just wanted to thank you. I mean, I know you haven't done anything yet, but I'd rather go down fighting. I don't want someone to kill me and then have to try and work out what happened once I'm dead."

"If you stick around as a ghost, you'd probably

have an easier time figuring out what happened. If you were already dead, I mean," I told her. Her face was drained of color. "No, no! Not that I'm encouraging you to choose that option. Just that we don't have a lot to work with since you're not sure what direction the threat is coming from."

"I've been thinking about this while sitting in there, and I really don't." Alice walked over to the patio table and sat down, staring out into the trees. "I mean, since my parents died? People have tried to take advantage of me. It's just the kind of thing that happens when you have money. I've had to be a little less trusting than I'd want to be." She looked up at me quickly and smiled. "I think that's why I like the pixie path."

"I can understand that."

"I didn't even know the uncle that left me all this," she said with a shrug. "Well, he left my parents this—my dad, to be specific—and then it came to me because they'd already passed away. My dad said he and his brother never got along, and he was as surprised as anybody when the lawyer showed up."

Archie and I looked at each other, surprise on our faces. "I'm sorry, I'm a little confused." I turned toward Alice. "How did your dad know the lawyer showed up if he had already passed away when you inherited?"

"It all happened really fast. It was just…It was fast." She looked down, her eyes tearing up. "He didn't even get a chance to enjoy it. He and mom were killed just a few weeks later."

That certainly didn't seem like an accident.

CHAPTER FIVE

"*I*was wondering when we were going to get another one of those star cards," Emma mused out loud while examining a giant, thick spiderweb hanging in the corner of the back porch. "It's almost like your goddess decided to give us a few weeks off to close all those cases. Right?"

"No. I doubt it works like that," I responded. I'd never known any powerful beings or pseudo-deities or potent paranormals with domineering tendencies to cut anyone else a break for compassion's sake.

Emma squinted at the large spider in the spiderweb. It stared quietly back at her. "You still don't really know how it works, Astra. So how would you know?" she pointed out without bothering to look me in the eye (which robbed me of the ability to make a face at her).

Emma Sullivan was sassy and salty and tough —which was, to be honest, a good part of the reason I liked her. It was also the only reason I let her comment pass without a stinging retort. No, I didn't know the intricacies and exactitudes of the star card, but I was sure it didn't build in vacation time.

"Anyway, Alice Windrow was not the person at the top of my list."

"You have a list of people in Forkbridge you think might be murdered?" Ami asked her.

"Yes. Well, no." Emma turned around swiftly, accidentally flinging her glass of ice water toward my sister. Ami winced and wiped droplets from her cheek. "I have a list of people I think might be murdered that some deity potentially could feel moved to save for various redeeming reasons." The detective took a sip of water. "I started thinking about it when Astra told me all about her sparkle cards."

"They're actually my sparkle cards," Ami replied, holding up her tarot deck. "Not Astra's."

I half-smiled at my younger sister's growing self-assurance.

"Fine. Your cards. Her sparkle. The owl's drama. The goddess's decree. Whatever." Emma waved her hand. "I don't care what any of it is, only that it's right. Anyway, they're not entirely horrible people—"

"Who?" I asked.

"—despite their repeated actions indicating that potential, and the risk of someone wanting them dead being naturally high, that's all." The detective raised her eyebrow. "It's a short list, really. I'll whip it out if anyone comes up."

"How are we going to handle this?" I asked Emma. "There's no crime, so I'm not sure how we get the police department officially involved in this. The captain seems pretty supportive of the whole 'psychic detective' thing, but there's no complaint. Not officially."

Emma gestured toward the patio doors. "Alice can make an official complaint."

"But against who?" Ami asked.

"No one. Just that there's been a general threat against her life."

"But there hasn't been," I told her. "Not from anyone."

"Of course there has. Didn't you and Ami just say that there was a threat against her life?" Emma set her water glass down and turned again toward the both of us. "We'll open up a case based on some nebulous potential threat that we don't specify. That'll allow us to get resources if we need them."

Ami's brow wrinkled with concern. "Can you do that?"

"Honey, I can do anything I want. Your sister and I just closed seventy-five old cases." Emma smirked. "For the moment, we're the 'it girls' in a department whose last 'it girl' was a miniskirted twenty-year-old intern in the evidence archives. Bless her heart, I don't think she ever did realize why all the officers wanted their evidence stored on the top shelf. The reasons had nothing to do with efficiency." She fixed my sister with an amused look. "If you get my drift."

Ami frowned.

"Do you know if there was ever any investigation done on the accident that killed Alice's parents?" I asked, trying to change the subject.

"No, I didn't check that, but as soon as you mentioned Alice Windrow, a name did pop into my mind immediately. Paul Wakefield." She looked back and forth. "You must not know he's been indicted over in Orlando for embezzlement. Seems a strange coincidence coming up right now, doesn't it?" Emma looked back and forth again, her eyebrows knitted together. "Really? Neither one of you have ever heard of him?"

We both shook our heads no.

"Paul Wakefield is the CEO of Punktex." A raised eyebrow. "Ringing any bells?"

"Punktex?" Ami's eyes widened. "Oh no, that's awful."

I looked back and forth, waiting for one of them to enlighten me. Still, apparently, my sister and the detective expected me to be previously enlightened. "What does a grocery chain have to do with Alice Windrow?"

Ami glanced at Emma. "Punktex is the grocery chain started by Alice's uncle. The one she didn't know?" Emma nodded. "I read about him in the newspaper occasionally before he died, but the chain is all over Florida."

"And several other states," Emma said. "It's huge."

I blew out a frustrated sigh. "So Alice runs this grocery chain?"

"No. Alice's money comes from this grocery chain," Emma told me. "But Alice doesn't run it. Well, technically, it may look like that, but…okay, see, it's privately owned. She's the chairman of the board of directors, but as far as I'm aware, that's the extent of her involvement." Emma leaned against a post. "I talked to the prosecutor in Orlando on the way over here, and they are pretty frustrated, actually. Alice is just completely unaware of what's going on with Paul. She, according to the prosecutor, doesn't want to admit he could be ripping her off, so the board isn't particularly cooperative with the investigation."

I narrowed my eyes. "Who's on the board of directors of Punktex?"

"Now you're getting it," Emma told me with a nod. "Alice Windrow and Paul Wakefield."

I blinked. "Just the two of them? No one else?"

"Yep. Just the two of them. It's private. They're not required to have more than that. She's got tons of money she inherited separate from Punktex, but the vast majority of her wealth is tied up in that grocery chain."

"The grocery chain this Paul Wakefield is being accused of embezzling from."

"Yep."

"Poor Alice," Ami murmured.

"Not poor," Emma disagreed. "She takes quite a bit of profit out of it. In fact, Punktex is technically the sponsor of this marathon, not Alice herself."

"So what happens if Alice Windrow dies before removing Paul Wakefield from the board?" I asked. "I mean, I'm assuming. I don't know much about corporate law, but since she's the owner, I'm guessing she can."

"It's a good guess. With just the two of them on the Board of Directors, Alice, as the owner, has ultimate control of Punktex. Unless—"

"Unless she dies," Ami whispered.

Emma nodded. "If she dies, he becomes the sole board member. If that happens, he's in full operational control of the company. Ultimately, it wouldn't matter who legally wound up owning it. The working papers say full control goes to him upon her death. That's it. The end. No contingency."

My jaw dropped. "Who would sign papers like that?"

Emma's eyes drifted toward the glass doors. "Her parents had just died. She just inherited Scrooge McDuck-level money and control of a company she only knew because that's where she grabbed her milk on the way home from aerobics." Emma turned back. "My guess? She signed whatever was put in front of her."

THE THREE OF us moved back inside to interrogate Alice Windrow, heiress and pixie follower. I felt vaguely unsettled by the case "assigned" to me by "Athena."

When I was in the paranormal military, I would've (no doubt) been assigned to defend the powerful Paul Wakefield had the situation been similar. I could have been tasked to find and arrest someone like Alice to get her out of the way. It wasn't unheard of. A CEO would have always trumped a twenty-something philanthropist with a pixie complex.

That's just how it was in my world.

Well. My previous world.

Well, the previous world, really. The Witches' Council was gone.

But it was hard not to recall how masterful my ultimate bosses were at exploiting people in their weakest moments for their own gain. I remembered their excitement when Charlotte Astley took over the Magical Midway—and how gleeful they were at the opening for attack, thanks to her uncle's demise. I watched them use Gunther Makepeace's sadness for the death of his mother against him.

So, sure. Considering the things I'd seen in my life?

I wasn't surprised someone was probably trying to exploit Alice Windrow. Something about Alice's personality made her seem defenseless, like a fluffy kitten that just wanted to chase a ball of yarn around until it was time for a nap. Because of that, though, this whole thing really annoyed me.

Only evil people exploit the defenseless.

And yet…it made me vaguely uncomfortable remembering some of the gentle, cuddly characters I'd thrown into paranormal prison because I was just following orders.

"Are you okay?" Ami asked, her quiet voice cutting into my thoughts. "Your face looks like you sucked on a lemon."

"I'm fine. I just get disgusted occasionally with humanity, and this is definitely one of those moments." My mother, Aunt Gwennie, and Archie sat around the kitchen table facing Alice. The owl leaned back and forth like a snake watching her, and the heiress laughed at his quick, flexible movements. "None of this should be happening to her."

"You can't say bad things shouldn't happen to anyone, Astra," Ami said, her voice low. "Life is all about balance. If we didn't know what the dark was, how could we appreciate the light? That's our purpose, you know."

I took a deep breath and turned, ready to rant at my naive sister and her unsophisticated way of looking at the world. My mother's lessons—holiday after holiday of the high priestess's countless spiritual justifications—echoed through Ami's words. It set my teeth on edge.

When something terrible happened to anyone, my mother would light a candle and pray softly to her goddess. Kneeling for hours, she would chant and beseech some powerful unseen deity to intercede, to change things. It wasn't quite "sitting in a room and cursing the darkness," but...well, to be frank, it wasn't chasing down a bad guy and slamming a lightning bolt up his butt, either.

Religion was nothing more than a soothing balm for people that needed a reason for suffering—and that was one reason I despised it.

I found my way of dealing with things practical.

I found my mother's way useless.

But...Ami wasn't my mother.

I exhaled slowly to deflate my offense before I put my sister on blast. "I know that's how you see things, Ami," I told her, keeping the judgment from my tone. "I just…don't."

"You don't what?" my mother asked.

"It's nothing, Mother," Ami answered for me, her voice suddenly subdued. "Astra and I were talking about something, that's all. It wasn't about Alice."

That subservience Ami displayed as soon as my mother opened her mouth? That natural stance of utter subjugation? It set my teeth on edge yet again. "Right. I think Emma has some questions for Alice, and we need to make a game plan for how we're going to handle this."

Before we could start, a bell rang from the store.

"I'll go see who it is," Aunt Gwennie said, jumping up. "You all stay here. This is much more important, and I know your mother is very interested in how you girls work through these situations. Aren't you, Minnie?"

My mother glanced toward Ayla, still lying on the couch, utterly ignoring the latest drama, and nodded quietly. "If you all wouldn't mind."

It wasn't a question.

She wore a pleasant expression as she glanced around the table as if we were her royal subjects, with her fierce eyes daring each of us to refuse her. I pulled up a chair and thought about all the times I had seen this show play out in my youth. Why bother saying no? What Mother wants, Mother gets. Her words could be polite, but her energy demanded compliance.

The thing is, though—this wasn't about my mother. Or me. Or the Ardens, really.

This was about Alice.

"It's really up to Alice how many people she wants to have as an audience to her interview, Mom," I answered without refusing. Ami froze as if she sensed the struggle for control between my mother and me before we'd even thrown down gauntlets. "If she only wants to talk to Emma privately, I think we should let her have that. This stuff is really personal, and maybe she doesn't want the entire Arden household knowing her business."

My mother stared at me, her face impassive.

"Oh, I don't mind," Alice answered in a chipper tone. "Astra, I've known your mom for years. Your whole family, really. And the pixies told me that I can trust her." She smiled at Mom. My mother turned, her expression filled suddenly with a disbelief writ large and loud across her face.

Mom and the pixies did not—and I mean did *not*—get along.

"But they hate her," Archie said without thinking.

My mother glared at the owl.

"I'm sure they don't hate her," I told Archie.

"Am I missing something?" Emma asked, her detective antenna sensing an untruth being set out on the table unexamined.

"You're fine. Let's just get started," I told her. She nodded.

THREE HOURS LATER, Detective Emma Sullivan scratched more thoughts in her case notepad as Alice went upstairs to nap. The questioning had been grueling and more than a little upsetting.

"Are you sure she can stay here?" Emma asked my mother, glancing up and then returning her gaze to the pad. "It would help, of course, but I don't want to put you guys out."

"Of course, though I don't know she'll be comfortable here. But it's either that or Astra goes and stays with her in her condo." My mother's usually confident face looked uncertain. "There was so much information shared. I don't know that I understand much more than I did when we started."

"Well, I understand a lot more than when we started, and that's all that matters, Mrs. A, since I'm the detective." Emma looked up briefly to smile reassuringly at her. "I know you all think this kind of stuff is predetermined, and you can look in a crystal ball and see what's going to happen—"

"Detective Sullivan," my mother said sharply, "if we thought we could do that, don't you think we would have done that already? Instead of sitting here for three hours while you pelted the poor girl with the most intimate of questions about her personal life?"

Emma didn't so much as flinch. "I meant no offense, Mrs. A."

"I am not married. I've never been married," Mom responded haughtily. "I'm not a Mrs. anyone, thank you."

Emma blinked that time. "Sorry, I just thought..." Her voice trailed off as she looked at me, then Ami. Finally, she glanced toward Ayla. Althea was off in the herb room buried in her potions, or Emma would have laid eyes on her, too. "I mean, you have four daughters that all look pretty similar to one another, so I just assumed you were divorced. Or a widow."

Minnie Arden, the high priestess of the goddess Athena and ruler of the Arden family coven, looked down her nose at Emma. The condescending look was so sharp, so unmistakable, and so well delivered, my mother practically looked British. "We don't marry in the Arden family."

"Right." Emma nodded. "Got it." She turned her body so my mother couldn't see her face and gave me a look that said she was apologetic for riling Mom but amused by my mother's arrogance. "Mom Arden is right, though, Astra. We can't let Alice go home alone. Not if we have no idea who's coming after her."

"You didn't narrow down anything from the interview?"

"Despite Alice's insistence that the pixies adore her, I can't rule out that this is paranormal in nature. I mean, the card came up, and that's paranormal, so…yeah, I mean…" Emma fell silent and gazed at her notes. "Thing is, though, I have no idea how to investigate a pixie. Or pixies." She sat up and looked at me. "Just go to the forest and ask a tree? I mean, how does this go?"

"I'll take care of that. The problem is I can't bring her."

"Her, who?"

"Alice. They may not be honest with me about what's going on with her if she's with me. And she needs to be guarded."

"I told you, Astra, she can stay here," my mother insisted again. "The house is warded."

Emma frowned. "What does that mean? Warded?"

"No one can come in this house with ill intentions toward anyone here," my mother responded, looking proud. "No weapon can cross, no attack can happen on these sacred grounds. This is a temple, after all." My mother frowned as Emma looked around like she was trying to spot which part of our house was an actual temple. "It's not about the decor, detective. It's about dedication and energy. Trust me, it's warded to be a sanctuary—"

"That doesn't extend to rabbits," Archie mentioned helpfully.

"It will the next full moon," Ami warned him.

Emma pulled out her service weapon and held it up. "I brought this in just fine. I don't think your wards work the way you think they do."

"You didn't come here to harm us," I told her.

"Try and shoot one of us," my mother suggested.

Emma blinked. "Pardon me?"

"Go on," Mom urged with a sly smile.

Emma appeared to consider the invitation but then shook her head no. "I can't do that. This is my service weapon. And, well…I could hurt you. Even if you say I won't, I just can't do that."

"I appreciate your ethics, detective, but your statement is more correct than you know. You can't do that. If you tried to shoot one of us, your gun would not go off. If it did, the bullet would not reach its intended target, I assure you."

Emma thought for a while, then holstered her gun. "I'm going to have to trust you because I'm not going to shoot you. I'd have to do the paperwork if I did, and man, that would be immense. I'm not in the mood. But it's good information to have for the future."

"In case you want to shoot me?" I asked.

Emma glared. "Don't push me, Arden."

CHAPTER SIX

The snakes and birds watched silently from the trees as we picked our way carefully into the swampy marshland.

"It just doesn't look like a pixie tracker."

"And what, pray tell, does a pixie tracker look like, human?"

"Don't be insulting," Emma mumbled.

"Calling you human is insulting?"

"Well, the way you say it, it didn't sound like a compliment." Emma stared at the small blue stone in the palm of my hand. No bigger than a quarter—more like a pebble, really—the smooth, glass-like sides glowed a soft blue. "I was expecting something much more ancient-looking. Maybe with a little steampunk flair." She squinted. "Though I'm beginning to get the idea you paranormals really like things that glow."

"You wouldn't be the first, the last, or the only person to have that opinion. I do need to point out, though, that energy makes light. Light glows. That's just science." Emma burst out laughing. "What?"

"You're holding a rock in your hand that's glowing blue, and we're following it into a swamp bog looking for pixies." She looked up at me. "I don't think science has anything to do with this, Astra." She pulled out a clear bottle with some kind of pink liquid in it and took a swig. "Man, it's hot."

"It is. Of course science has something to do with it. Magic is just natural stuff that science hasn't explained yet."

"You're the most pragmatic witch I've ever met."

"And how many witches have you met?"

"I would have said six—your family—but considering some of the stories you've told me about how many of you there are? Who knows."

"Watch out," I told her, pointing.

As Emma stepped around a swampy puddle

with ominous air bubbles, her yellow plastic boots made obscene sucking sounds in the mud. "Ugh. This is so gross." She looked at my sleek black boots. "How are your feet not getting wet?"

"Magic. Now be quiet." The stone pulsed a deeper hue of blue. "When it starts pulsing like that, it means we're close."

Our lack of trust in the pixies had dictated that a meeting topped the list. She insisted we take her sleeper Malibu death trap—even though I was pretty sure my Jeep would have been a far more practical choice to hunt pixies. When the tracking stone brought us to the edge of a swamp just north of Forkbridge proper, I resisted the urge to remind her my 4x4 could have driven right into the thing.

"Ugh, it's so humid in here." Emma slapped at a mosquito. A frog croaked in reply. "And if there's this many frogs, how are there still so many mosquitos?"

"Just pray we get in and out of here before dusk. There'll be swarms of the things all over us, and it won't only be mosquitos." I took a step but slipped and lost my footing.

Emma's arm shot out and grabbed my shoulder. "Whoa, I got you!" She thrust me toward a black-trunked tree for further support. The tracker rock pulsed white, and I put my finger to my lips. "They're close enough to see us," I whispered.

"Um, Astra?" Emma pointed toward the tree.

I turned and came face-to-face with a snake just inches from my nose. I blinked. He blinked. I blinked. His forked tongue flicked out and tasted the air.

"Shoo, dude."

The snake gave me a bored, disinterested look and slithered up the tree slowly.

Emma whistled. "Aren't you afraid of anything?"

I made a dismissive gesture. "I've made a career out of not being scared of things. I mean, I have a healthy fear of the unknown, just enough to make sure I'm cautious and not stupid. But is there anything that can freeze me in fear?" I shrugged. "Not that I've come across yet."

"Good, because there's an alligator behind you," Emma told me calmly.

"Is he attacking?"

She shook her head no.

"Then we're probably fine. The gator couldn't bite through my uniform if he tried, anyway."

"What's this 'we' thing, Astra?" The detective

eyed the area behind me warily. "I'm not wearing the fang-proof Black Widow cosplay magic armor. If he can't chomp your leg off, he just might come for me."

"He won't, and if he does, I'll—" I stopped and stared at the rock. It shone bright white, steady. Once the rock stopped pulsing, it could only mean one thing. "The pixies are here."

"Where?" Emma whispered back. She glanced up in the trees.

"Look down. They're tiny and wingless."

"Rude," a high-pitched voice said faintly from the direction of my feet.

THE SMILING pixie looked up at me, his green hair wild as it cascaded over his pointed ears and onto his stout shoulders. He looked like a gym rat troll doll. "My name is Pistachio Waterflash. I am Chieftain of the Forkbridge pixies." All seven inches of him tried to look tough as he thrust out his bare, muscled chest and tilted his head. "You must be Astra Arden. Ebony said you would be coming."

"Oh, my gosh, he's smaller than a Barbie doll," Emma said, her eyes wide.

"A few inches shorter, yes," he answered, craning his neck. Placing his tiny, barely perceptible hands on his hips, he smiled coyly up at her. "I can assure you, however, I am much more functional than a Ken doll, lovely Emma." The tone made it sound like his statement was accompanied by wiggling eyebrows, but to tell you the truth, they were so small I couldn't tell for sure.

Emma blinked. "How do you know my name?"

"We have heard tell of—AH!" Pistachio shouted and dove to the ground as a dark form dove from the sky.

"Archie!"

Archie barely missed grabbing the tiny pixie with his sharp talons.

The pixie scrambled under a downed branch and peaked out fearfully. "Are you barmy, man?" he squeaked in indignation. Turning to me, he shrieked, "You brought an owl here?"

"I am the goddess's own owl, you nutter! Of course I came with them!" Archie flew down and landed on a dead tree limb. Leaning forward, he clicked his beak at Pistachio. "Why would you walk around seven inches tall in a swamp with predators?"

"Because it's our swamp, you arrogant prat!" the pixie shouted back with a distinct southern accent. "Bloody plonker! Get out of our swamp!"

"Make me, inchworm," Archie told him ominously.

Emma looked confused. "Why is he talking like he watches too much BBC?"

I looked up. "Pixies are from England." It was an odd thing, to be sure, but all pixies I'd ever met had an impressive repertoire of British insults. It was like they had a pixie playbook with them all listed, passed down from generation to generation.

Her confusion remained. "But he doesn't have an accent."

"I'm not from our homeland," Pistachio sniffed. "My family originated from there. We got stuck on a ship several hundred years ago."

"Okay, got it." Emma did not look like she got it.

"Come on out, shorty, let's play," Archie told Pistachio, his feathers ruffling with heightened excitement. "Let's see who's faster." Archie narrowed his eyes. "I bet it's me."

"Archie! Stop that!"

"You just know he's the reason Alice is in danger," Archie warned me, glaring at the pixie again with a threatening posture. "Let's just eat him now so I can hunt some frogs. We'll be done with this. Maiden saved, owl fed. I mean, what a night, right?"

"Oh, bollocks," Pistachio said under his breath (which meant I could barely, just barely, hear him). Pistachio Waterflash stepped out from under the branch with a final menacing glare at my owl and began to glow.

"Does everything glow?" Emma muttered.

Within a few seconds, the pixie was ten inches, then twelve inches, then two feet. Within a minute, Pistachio stood in front of us as tall as any normal-sized man. He still looked otherworldly with his shock of long, bright green hair and shirtless chest thrust out proudly. "Perhaps this is better?" He smiled widely. "Ladies. Welcome to my bog."

"Oh my goodness," Emma breathed. She sniffed the air, looked at Pistachio, then stepped closer and sniffed again. "You smell like the woods after a summer rain." She blinked. "Is that a cologne?"

I tried not to laugh. Emma looked thunderstruck.

Pistachio smiled at her and stretched his muscles like a sunbathing cat waking up from a nap. "It is not, fair Emma." Now deep and smolderingly sexy, his voice seemed to cast an even more penetrating spell on Emma, and she gulped loudly. "This is the natural scent of the pixie. We are of nature, and so the scent of nature clings to us like—"

"Oh, for goodness sake, stop talking like you're the star of a Shakespearean play, would you?" Archie snorted as he flew toward Pistachio and whacked him in the head with his wing. "No one's impressed by you, you walking Ken doll."

"Would you like to see how much I am not like a Ken doll?" Pistachio retorted, reaching to untie the drawstring of his bright red shorts.

"Okay, gentlemen, can we stop with the—" I stopped myself, looked at the two, and gave up on classifying whatever was going on between them. The only words I could think of wouldn't be polite to say in mixed company and, to be frank, with Pistachio now at this size? He would absolutely win any measuring contest. "Whatever this is, let's just stop it. Pistachio, we're here to find out if the pixies have marked Alice Windrow for death." I crossed my arms. "Have they? Have you?"

He blinked, a shocked look on his face. "Why would we mark her for death? She honors us."

"How so?" Emma asked, her eyes drifting toward Pistachio's chiseled chest. "How does a human honor a pixie man—um, a pixie?"

"She brings us gooseberries shipped from England," he answered, a dreamy look sliding across his face. "I don't know how she manages it, but their tart, juicy flavor..." Pistachio's look of ecstasy was nearly obscene.

I cleared my throat. No response. "Um. Pistachio?"

With a sigh, his face cleared, and he looked slightly more present. "We would never do anything to hurt that wonderful, benevolent woman. I assure you, goddess-hand."

He looked at me with enough admiration to make me blush. "What did you call me?"

"Goddess-hand," Pistachio answered, smiling. "Years ago, we would have called you handmaiden, but since that Hulu show?" He tsk-tsked and looked sadly at both Emma and me—as if extending sympathy for our state of being female. "Entirely different connotation now, isn't it?" The pixie tossed his green hair over his shoulder, quite Fabio-like, and glared at Archie. "Shame the bright-eyed one couldn't get you better help."

"Hey, who you callin' the help, bub?" the owl thundered.

"If Alice is a follower," Emma asked quickly to head off another explosion between the bird and the chieftain, "why are you all not protecting her? Since she follows the pixie path, don't you owe her some level of safeguarding?"

"We could give her asylum here in the swamp," Pistachio answered with a nod, "but this is the only place we have ultimate control. Most humans are not particularly enthusiastic about living in a swamp teeming with alligators and mosquitos and snakes and frogs." Pistachio Waterflash stepped to stand in front of Emma and gazed down at her, his eyes shining with mischief. He grinned as he caught sight of her delicate blush. "Even if we would have the ultimate control to give them joy and safety beyond measure." Pistachio reached forward and grazed her arm with the tips of his fingers.

I did my best not to snicker.

Archie?

Archie did not.

The owl exploded with laughter. "Whoah, boy. Does that actually work? 'Hey, baby, come visit me at my dank, stinky, muddy swamp so I can control you with my extra big ears. They're so big

I pick up streaming services!' What a crock!" The owl laughed even harder as the pixie whirled to face him, an angry look darkening his usually joyous expression. "You're a hoot, Pistachio. A real hoot!"

"Get out!" the pixie chieftain roared. "I will not be insulted in my own realm!"

I scrambled forward and reached toward him. "I'm really sorry—"

He whirled on me before I could bow or scrape. "You as well. I have answered your questions. I have no quarrel with you, but your flea-bitten bird has no sense of respect. You brought him here. Now you and he must go. Get him far from my sight before he's eaten by an alligator."

All around us, water splashed. I glanced to find several alligators floating closer and closer and closer. More eyes broke the water's surface like submarines setting up for an attack.

"We'll go." He nodded, looking satisfied. "And I'm sorry that Archie disrespected you, Chieftain. Truly I am. Thank you for answering our questions."

He considered me and then nodded, accepting my apology as sincere. Turning toward Emma, Pistachio smiled once again, all sexy-like. "You may stay, fair Emma." He leaned forward and placed his face close to her hair, and breathed deeply. "Your scent, like honey, is quite pleasing to me."

Oh, dear lord.

Emma looked up at him and blinked once, then twice. It was as if the hardened detective was trying to process the absurd unreality of the situation.

I couldn't help but notice Pistachio stood between Emma and the path out of the swamp. Not…blocking her. Not stopping her. Just subtly clarifying he didn't want her to go.

"Hey, enough with—" Archie began, but the big-mouthed bird soon found my thumb and forefinger pinching his deadly rabbit-killing beak closed. I was lucky I didn't lose a finger.

"Be quiet," I whispered. "Not everything needs running commentary from you."

The owl stared at me, his eyes angry. But he didn't struggle.

"I WANTED TO STAY," Emma told me as she drove exceedingly, frustratingly slow toward town. "That was just bizarre. Like, I wanted to stay. I wanted to blow off my job, pack up my apartment, and just stay in the swamp with him."

"Um-hmm," I answered noncommittally.

"Would a pixie lie?" she asked.

"About Alice being marked for death? No, I don't think so. He has no reason to, really— Pistachio is a Chieftain, after all. He's pixie royalty. He wouldn't have any reason to think we'd be able to stop him, much less that we would put in the effort."

"Right, no, yeah, about Alice. That's good."

I stared at her. "Were you not asking about Alice?"

Emma blushed hotly. "No, I was."

"You were not! You want to know if Pistachio was sincere in his completely over-the-top flirtation."

"Was he flirting?" Emma asked distractedly. "I just figured he was being friendly. You know, hospitable. Maybe trying to get a new human worshiper or something." She ran her hand through her damp hair.

"Pixies are not smoldering sexpots, Emma. They do things for people, but they're not some tiny, seven-inch tall sex cult or something. They like gifts, they like to give gifts, and they like people to be happy. They're more likely to find you a boyfriend than flirt with you," I told her.

"So that was—"

"You were hit on by the pixie chieftain."

"No, that can't be right."

"You were there. What would you call it?" I asked her as casually as I could

"Overwhelming," she breathed. "I think I heard bells. I've never felt that kind of pull toward anyone before. It was…otherworldly."

"You wouldn't be the first or the last human to be attracted to a paranormal," I told her as we turned down my street. "I've heard it can be overwhelming, and those relationships can work. If it didn't, there wouldn't be so many psychic humans running around. But one thing you do have to keep in mind."

"What's that?"

"He's a chieftain." Nothing in Emma's face demonstrated this news changed her way of thinking one way or the other. "Their leader?" Still nothing. "The chieftain dating a human won't be popular, Emma. The wife of the chieftain is an honored position—"

"Wait a minute, wait a minute, wait. Wife?" Emma's wide eyes shot toward me, looking crazed. "Slow down there, speedy. I'm not marrying a freaking pixie. For one, when I dreamed about the places I would live as an adult, swamp never came up anywhere on the list. Two?" Emma took a deep breath. Then she exhaled loudly. "Look, forget the list. You're just jumping way, way ahead of the curve here, my friend."

"I just think people should be fully informed before they careen off a cliff, you know? No judgment here. Just saying." I turned and looked out the window. The slow crawl of the car was only one of the outward indications that meeting Pistachio had rattled Emma. I'd never seen her like this.

"I'm not careening off a cliff."

"Not at this speed, no. Old lady Smith just passed us on her late afternoon walk, and I think she's at least ninety."

The Malibu crept slowly into the driveway, and Emma put it in park. "Look, either way, we don't think the pixies are after Alice, so that means it's plain old human murder."

I nodded. "I think so."

"Well, since greed is usually a highly motivating factor in most evil human endeavors, I say we start focusing on Paul Wakefield, pronto. Let's just not think about Pistachio Waterflash and his pectoral muscles for a while." Emma looked at me. "Deal?"

"Deal." I raised my eyebrow. "But I didn't say anything about the pixie's pecs."

"Shut up, Astra."

CHAPTER SEVEN

"Who hat was that back there?"

Archie stared. He looked innocent and sweet. Even charming. But the murderous raptor wasn't fooling me. "What was what?" He blinked.

"Dude."

"My lady." The owl bowed regally.

I'd finally found the cantankerous owl in the far right corner of the backyard sitting (hiding) in Ayla's old treehouse. While Emma toiled away in the main house looking for information on Paul Wakefield and my sisters worked with Aunt Gwennie to prepare dinner, it seemed a perfect time to ask the bird why he was such a jerk.

"You swooped down on the pixie chieftain. A

chieftain, mind you, we had found to ask for his help." I told him. He stared back like I was talking about someone else. "Do you have any idea the kind of problems we'd have if you ate a chieftain? What the heck were you thinking?"

"First, I wasn't going to eat the pistachio; I just wanted to crack his shell a little bit." Archie ruffled out his feathers inside the small makeshift window. "The pixie path," he scoffed. "You realize there is no pixie path, right?"

"What does it matter? Alice feels there is, and who are you to judge, anyway? That's a reason to grab a pixie in your talons?"

"Pixies have no serious magic other than pooping out pixie dust. They're not gods. This pixie path is just something they made up to get humans to bring them things. Has to be. The whole thing is manipulation, I tell you. Like a cult." The owl put one wing on his hip and pointed the other wing out the window. "Pistachio Waterflash is nothing more than a con man."

While Archie was exaggerating about the pixies being essentially useless, he wasn't entirely wrong regarding their magical capabilities. Pixies had limited magical power—they could make areas safe sanctuary for themselves. Any animals that lived within that area would respect their rule or leave, but that was more politeness than anything else. They could make—not poop—pixie dust (which, despite the modern myths of *Peter Pan*, doesn't make you fly—it shrinks you down to pixie size).

The owl looked aggravated that I was unmoved by his passionate statements. "So what? We didn't go there for that. We went there for his help." No response. "Archie, why do you care? They're not hurting anybody."

"That you know of." Archie frowned, then clicked his beak. "Elemental con men." The agitated owl paced in the window.

His reaction to them was baffling, but this wasn't the first time the owl's dislike of a species or creature baffled me. First the parrots in Parrot Paradise, and now the pixies. I wasn't sure if his dislike of the pixies was based on some reality I didn't yet know about, or I was simply discovering my owl had a prejudice problem.

Who could dislike pixies? I mean, they were just earth fairies, right?

Maybe I should explain.

There are four main fairy types.

Fairies (or air fairies, the ones with wings)—they could shrink down and fly, but, for the most part, they lived their lives at average size in paranormal towns. Pixies (or earth fairies) could become normal-sized but generally lived in their teeny-tiny state. Salamanders (or fire fairies)—again, much like air fairies—could shrink down but typically don't. Then there were mermaids (or water fairies) who, obviously, live in the ocean and are rarely seen.

Yes, there are more branches of the fairy family, like brownies or sylphs, but those groups branched off from these four types.

Now, each elemental group had some shared characteristics with their element—the air fairies could be flighty and whimsical, the fire fairies could be destructive and volatile, the water fairies could be calm, or...well, you get the point.

I know what you're thinking.

Earth elementals would seem to be steady, constant. Right?

Think again.

Is a volcano steady?

How about an earthquake?

Archie's wild accusations and lousy behavior aside, I knew from my military training that pixies could be deceptively calm. Deceptively innocent. Problems with them could show up with such subtlety, it was possible not to see them coming at all. By the time you realize they're actually hellbent on destruction, the explosion's usually past stopping.

"Look, I'm not dismissing what you're saying out of hand, but I am trying to understand. You sound like a speciesist giving me nothing but hyperbole because you don't like pixies. That's all I'm getting." I shifted in the tiny tree house and pulled my legs underneath me. "Right now, it sounds to me like you're just annoyed a non-god paranormal decided to start a spiritual path. Just because the pixie isn't a god doesn't make him the leader of a cult or that path destructive."

He stopped and looked at me. "It does sound like that, and I am annoyed about that," Archie deadpanned. "But it's not some jealous god thing. It's more than that. I was fine with the idea of a pixie path. I mean, sure—who doesn't need a little more giggles in their life, right?"

"That's what I thought."

The bird again paced back and forth on the rough window sill. "But when I saw that flamboyant, smarmy pixie with his flowing green hair and bedroom eyes, when I heard his oily 'you smell like honey, baby, come stay in my swamp'?"—Archie's feathers curled up at the end of his wings like he was balling up the fists he didn't have—"I wanted to pelt him with owl pellets."

Ew. "You attacked him before he ever did that, though," I pointed out. "And you basically said you attacked him for being short. Out of nowhere. Archie, it looked petty and completely arbitrary." He stopped pacing. "Was it?" The owl waved his wing and shrugged. "Archie?" My eyes narrowed as the silent refusal to answer dragged out even longer. "What are you not telling me here?"

Archie's expression clouded with guilt for about two seconds, and then the guilt melted into a poker-faced mask. It was like watching an anthropomorphized cartoon owl morph back into the mysterious, inscrutable animal he was inspired by. "I don't know what you're talking about. Why would I withhold information from you?"

I gave him a doubting look—verging on suspicious.

I liked Archie. I even mostly trusted him.

But I'd learned the hard way most people lie. Most people operate off their own agenda— agendas that don't always necessarily align with mine. As the two of us stared at one another in the sunset's orange glow, I wondered if Archie had an agenda I didn't know about.

"THE OWL'S lying to me. At least, I think the owl is lying to me," I announced to Emma. When she didn't look up, I pulled out a chair and straddled it backward. "Mom?" I called toward the kitchen. "Does Athena have any particular problem with pixies? Any reason Archie would dive-bomb a pixie chieftain in a swamp with absolutely no provocation and then refuse to tell me why he did it?"

"You're assuming there was no provocation," Emma pointed out without looking up.

"No, I'm saying it looked like there was no provocation, and when asked, the owl refused to tell me if there was. I'm also assuming the goddess Athena exists in this scenario, which is a stretch."

Her brow furrowed. "There must have been some provocation for it. I just can't see Archie wanting to hurt Pistachio. I can't see anyone wanting to hurt him, really."

I looked at her. "We were both there, though," I told her, surprised. "There was no provocation."

From Emma's perspective, Archie was simply an owl. She knew that he could speak to us and we to him, but she didn't have any direct relationship with him. Where was this opinion he wouldn't attack the pixie coming from?

"He was hungry, and he doesn't care who he kills?" My sister Ami thrust her head into the dining area. "I mean, that would be my guess. Since the brute regularly rips apart Peter Cottontail in the garden."

"Now, Ami, Archie is still part of the natural world, and we have to respect that," Aunt Gwennie admonished my sister. She passed by Ami in the doorway to set down a stack of plates on the table. "Whatever else he is, he's still an owl. I wouldn't judge any of you for eating what you're meant to eat. You shouldn't judge him."

"Whatever," Ami muttered.

"Speaking of eating, we're having stuffed flounder tonight. I hope you'll be joining us, Emma." Aunt Gwennie looked at my friend affectionately, but Emma's nose was buried in her computer, and she didn't respond.

"Look, I'm not judging him for eating."

"No, your sister was," Aunt Gwennie gestured toward Ami.

I rolled my eyes. "He tried to attack Pistachio

Waterflash, and he won't tell me what motivated him to do it." I tapped the chair. "He's hiding something from me, and I want to know what it is."

Emma looked up from her laptop at the mention of the sexy pixie's name. "Pistachio Waterflash? Is he here?"

Before I could answer, Alice perked up on the couch and turned her attention from the television.

"Pistachio is here?" Alice looked around. "Where? Is he coming for dinner?"

I looked back and forth between the two women. "No. He's not here."

Emma and Alice exchanged a long look, and then they both sighed.

Aunt Gwennie and I exchanged looks. What the heck?

I turned toward Emma. "What is it with you and the pixie?" I asked, my voice low. "I know he's cute and flirty, and the pecs were easy on the eyes, but you've been in a haze ever since you met the guy. It's like you're under a spell or something." I raised my eyebrow. "Are you under a spell or something?"

Althea, who had been walking by with a salad, stopped and turned to consider Emma with practiced eyes. The quiet potion master's gaze swept up and down and back around again as if she was ticking off a checklist in her head.

"I know, I have been a little. I told you, Astra. He was just so overwhelming." Emma shifted in her chair, tilted her laptop screen, and pointed toward it. "I've been reading about the myths around pixies, and none of them—"

"Wait a minute. You've been doing what?" I stared at her.

"Reading about pixies."

She was supposed to be in here looking up information on Paul Wakefield. In fact, shifting the investigation to him and immediately diving in was her idea. Not mine. Instead, she's been googling pixie pages?

"Why are you looking at information about pixies?"

"I just told you. Wait. What do you mean?" Emma asked, frowning.

"Did you get done with the Paul Wakefield stuff? We decided that's where we were going to shift our focus." I paused, waiting for an answer. Emma didn't respond. "Well, it's where you decided you would shift your focus. Remember?" Nothing. "Paul Wakefield? Embezzler? CEO of

Punktex? Alice Windrow's life being in danger? Glow star card? Any of this ringing a bell?"

"Paul who?" Emma's eyes looked unfocused.

I looked at Althea with alarm.

"I get the reason for the expression, and there's clearly something"—Althea swept her hand in a circle toward Emma—"going on, but there's no tell-tale definitive sign I can spot to tell me exactly what it is."

"Can you take a guess?" Aunt Gwennie asked.

"If I'd met her on the street? I'd just say she was in love. Elevated heart rate, pupils slightly dilated, but all just...slight. Nothing major. Not enough to be artificially induced, and nothing to explain the brain fog that seems to have her in its grip." Althea tilted her head. "Everything I'm seeing could all be completely natural in the right circumstances."

"Could it be magically induced?" I asked.

"That's probably a better question for Mom." Althea was an incredibly disciplined witch for a fifteen-year-old. She knew what her expertise was in, and she knew when to stay in her lane and refer something out. She would've done well in the potion department of the military.

"You're probably right. Where is Mom?"

Althea looked around. "Weren't you talking to her a minute ago?"

"I asked her about the pixies earlier, but she never answered." I glanced at everyone and took a quick mental roll call. Ami, Althea, and Ayla were here. Aunt Gwennie was in the kitchen. Alice sat on the couch staring at the television, and Emma at the table googling pixie pictures. I didn't see Archie, but he was probably still sulking in the treehouse. "Has anyone seen Mom?"

"Maybe upstairs?" Althea glanced at me. "I'll go check."

"I've got it." I got up and turned toward the stairway. "Can you do me a favor and just keep an eye on Emma and Alice?"

"Sure. I can do that."

I FOUND my mother sitting in the parlor of the two-room suite she shared with Aunt Gwennie, seated in a wing chair. Her finger rested on her chin, and her eyes looked off into space. "Mom?"

Her pale eyes focused on me. "Yes, Astra?"

"What are you doing here?" The perfectly innocuous question came out like a threat, and her eyes widened at my tone. I held my hands up quickly. "I'm sorry. I know how that came out. I'm sorry. I've just developed this way of speaking that sounds way more confrontational than I think it does. I'm sorry."

"Yes, well, as a high priestess, I can sympathize with the tone of authority invading conversations even when it has no place." She patted the chair next to her. "Come, Astra, sit down. Maybe if you're not towering over me looking down at me, your tone will soften a bit. Little ritualistic changes can have that effect."

I moved across the room and sat down. "What are you doing up here all alone?" I made it sound less like an accusation and more like a genuine question of concern. "Everybody's downstairs, and dinner is almost ready."

Silvery threads of gray snaked through her hair. I noticed lines under her eyes, around her mouth. I wasn't sure if they were from age or exhaustion. Mom had always seemed larger-than-life to me, the strong authority and center of our family. Now she looked slightly old, a little tired. Even her hair was a bit dull.

"I was just up here thinking, Astra. Thinking about how far you girls have come." Her eyes moved back toward the window. "I am heartened—more than you could possibly know

—that you are forming a genuine bond with your sisters."

"I'm pretty happy about it, too. Honestly. They're cool."

Mom turned and looked at me. "The goddess was absolutely brilliant in giving you Archie for your birthday. The job she's given you has given all of them purpose, too." Her eyes burned with intensity, and she added quietly, "I know you think I did all this, but I'm not as smart as Athena."

"Mom, you sound a little odd," I said with concern. "Is everything okay?"

She waved away my suddenly anxious expression. "I'm just getting older, Astra, and when you get older, you start to take stock of your life. Choices you've made that, perhaps, weren't the best ones. The guilt you chose not to feel comes back many years later, as if you transgressed just yesterday. Karma always comes home to roost."

I said nothing. I wasn't sure what to say.

Suddenly, my mom's expression cleared. "I am truly sorry for the way I treated you when you told me you wanted to go into the military. Had I known the rift between us would last fifteen years, I never would've said what I said. I should've listened more. I'm sorry, and I am sorry that you and your sisters' relationships suffered for my…my inability to find my way through in a way that preserved those ties."

Now I really wasn't sure what to say.

The tension blanketing the air every time my mother and I walked into a room together had ebbed and flowed since I returned. My own silent mental responses to her arrogant pronouncements of late had been…Well, let's just say I felt myself slipping back into a pattern of dismissing her, just as I heard her tone falling back into a habit of dismissing me. "I didn't handle it well either, Mom. It wasn't just you."

"Yes, but you were a child, and it was my responsibility as the adult—"

"I wasn't really a child, mom."

"Of course you were."

"I was old enough to join the paranormal military. That's hardly a child."

A smile crept across her face. "You just have to argue with me, don't you?"

"I'm not arguing, I'm—" I stopped myself.

The two of us chuckled.

If I had to do it all over again, I'd have done the same thing. I didn't feel I was wrong choosing to pursue the life that I wanted to lead, regardless of my mother's permission. I didn't need her permission to be myself or to select the path of my life.

But I didn't try very hard before I left to help her understand why I needed to do it and what it was about military life that appealed to me.

And once I left, I didn't try at all.

"Perhaps we can put this aside until Alice's safety is secured," Mom said, the intimacy that had been woven in her words now gone. "What was it you needed from me?"

"Do you know anything about pixies?" I asked.

"Enough. What's the problem?"

"Emma and Alice both met the pixie chieftain, Pistachio Waterflash, and now they're both acting like...I don't know. Weird. Almost like obsessed teenagers with a crush. I don't know Alice at all, but for Emma? The way she's acting is completely out of character."

Mom made a face, and I couldn't tell whether it was one of concern or dismissal. The high priestess cloak had wrapped around her once again, and her reactions were difficult to read. "Anything else?"

"Archie dive-bombed Pistachio back at the swamp with no warning, and he won't tell me why."

CHAPTER EIGHT

It was almost dinnertime when Mom and I emerged on the first floor. The broiled fish scent made my mouth water, but the sight of a giggling Emma and a coquettish Alice seated on the floor in front of the laptop screen made my jaw drop. "I think Pistachio is way hotter than this pixie," Emma told Alice with a wrinkle of her nose. "I mean, these pictures all make them look like children."

Alice wiggled her eyebrows. "Pistachio's no child, right?" The two women leaned into one another, clasping hands, and snickered as if they shared a secret no one else knew. "I don't think I've ever seen anyone as handsome as him. And he never wears a shirt. Was he wearing a shirt when you met him? Please tell me he wasn't wearing a shirt."

"Nope. He wasn't wearing one when I met him," Emma breathed. Her eyes widened as if suddenly remembering something. "Did you see his pectoral muscles? They were unbelievable. Like a chiseled statue." The detective's blush deepened with vivid color. "It was all I could do to keep from putting my hands on them and just squeezing."

"If you're wondering—and I have no doubt that you are—yes, this has been going on a while," Althea deadpanned warily.

"See what I mean?" I glanced at my mother. "What have you got by way of explanation for this embarrassing display?"

Mom stared at the two, astonished. "Grown women regressed to lovesick teenagers?" Mom crossed her arms and examined the two with a puzzled frown. "Althea was right. There's nothing obviously wrong with either one of them. Usually, those enchanted by a magical creature have a bit of an otherworldly glow I can see. There is none here. Or if there is, it's so subtle that I can't pick up on it."

I raised an eyebrow. "That's useful. Can anyone see this?"

Mom glanced at me and nodded. "With a lot of practice, sure."

"I smelled their breath," Althea told our mother. "There wasn't anything there that indicated either one of them had ingested anything. At least, nothing I could detect that would explain this."

We stared as if Emma and Alice were specimens on display in a laboratory. At the same time, the scent of seasoned fish grew stronger. "I do have a radical idea," Mom said, gesturing toward the two. "Have you asked them why they are like this? Emma in particular, since you're more familiar with her?"

"Obviously, we thought of that. Astra asked her what was wrong with her," Althea said with a hint of annoyance at my mother's question. "It was one of the first things she did, actually. Emma didn't acknowledge the question. Not really."

"Maybe we should start with Archie," Mom suggested. "He may be stubborn, but at least he still has his wits about him. It doesn't look to me like the two of them do anymore." Emma and Alice tittered girlishly again to illustrate Mom's point.

Just then, Emma's cell phone rang.

She ignored it as if she wasn't a detective, and that call had no chance of being about anything important. Like a murder.

It rang again.

She ignored it again.

When Emma showed no signs of interrupting her pixie fandom squealing session with Alice, I raced over to the table and checked the caller ID. "Crap. It's the station." I tapped the screen. "This is Astra Arden on Detective Emma Sullivan's phone. How can I help you?"

"Astra?" It was Chief Harmon. "What are you doing with Emma's phone?"

"Hiya, Chief. Emma's in a...meeting with Alice Windrow about the marathon coming up in a few days," I said on the fly without thinking. A lie is always easier to remember if there was a grain of truth. "Alice just wanted an outside opinion about the security challenges."

"She's talking to Emma about this?" Chief Harmon asked. "Why would Ms. Windrow talk to Emma about security for her marathon? Isn't Punktex taking care of all that?"

"Yeah, probably, but she knew that Emma had been in Afghanistan and...well, come on, Chief, you know how two women get when they run into each other and want an excuse to sit and gab." My mother gave me a sharp look from across the room, and I held up my hands silently in frustration. Yes, what I just said was a female stereotype and not a very accurate one, but it was the best I could do in the moment. "I'm sure they're just talking about hairstyles or something."

"Right, that makes sense," he answered, satisfied.

I rolled my eyes. The reason stereotypes are so effective is that people swallow them hook, line, and sinker without questioning. Not necessarily a good thing, but it helped me out this very moment.

"The reason I'm calling is that we've had a report of some vandalism at a construction site on the southern edge of town."

"Why does vandalism need a detective?" I asked. "Wouldn't that be more appropriate for a patrolman?"

"You know you're not even really a police officer, right, Ms. Arden?" the chief shot back, bristling at my question. "How about you leave the actual law enforcement to me?"

Well, because had I done that, all your cold cases would still be open.

I cleared my throat.

"Right, sorry, chief," I told him apologetically.

"Can you two check it out? I need her to work on this pronto."

"Do you need me to get her out of the meeting?" I asked, praying to whatever deity could hear me he answered no. I could cover for Emma pretty easily, but if she got on the phone with the chief acting the way she was? He wouldn't think she was possessed or enchanted. He would think she was on drugs and would probably suspend her.

"No, that's not necessary. I'll send the location and information to the app. I just wanted to touch base with her to let her know this case might be slightly related to a case she was asking about going on in Orlando." It sounded like the chief was shuffling papers on his desk. "One of the major investors in this property is Paul Wakefield, and he—"

"He was arrested for embezzling from Punktex, wasn't he?" I asked, glancing at Alice.

"Arrested, but not indicted yet," the chief responded. "Since we don't know whether he actually did it or whether he's actually going to prison for it, I'd like Emma to handle this with kid gloves. Paul's still a citizen in our town, and if they don't throw him in prison, we're going to have to live with him for a long time." The chief cleared his throat. "Now, I'm not telling Emma to give him any special treatment, but let's handle this…carefully."

It always amused me when politicians made political statements they tried to ensure wouldn't be seen as political statements. The directive to handle a vandalism case by the force's top detective and to do it carefully? That was the chief telling Emma to give him special treatment.

"I will pass it all on to her, Chief."

I hit the screen to hang up and stared at my partner. "Well, it seems I've got a problem," I told my mother.

IF THERE'S one thing a coven of witches is good at, it's figuring out how to cover all angles of a problem. That goes double for a coven of witches all related.

"Aunt Gwennie and I will hit the books and see if we can find some historical precedent for pixies doing whatever this is to people," Mom told me. "Althea and Ayla can help keep an eye on the two of them to make sure nothing happens." Mom looked around. "But before I do that, I'm going to find Archie and see if I can find out what's going on with him and his dislike of Pistachio."

"And why he's not telling me," I added.

"Well, he may not tell me anything, but I am Athena's high priestess. Hopefully, that confers some sort of top-secret clearance as far as the owl is concerned."

"But I'm the star...Um, the star thing." I still had no idea what to call myself. "I should get to know whatever the owl knows."

"Yes, dear, you are the star thing," Mom agreed, her solemn forehead smoothing into a lack of expression. "No one is telling you you're not the star thing."

"Minnie, stop teasing her," Aunt Gwennie chided.

My mother half-grinned. "She makes it so easy, Gwennie." Mom winked at me. "Look, the owl didn't arrive in this house with a handbook. He's not your familiar, exactly, so we don't really know what the rules are regarding him. Is there something he knows that he technically can't tell you because of some guidelines Athena set out for what you need to do on your own? Is he throwing a hissy fit to try and get it across without breaking the rules that he has to follow?"

Mom shrugged. "We don't know, but it wouldn't surprise me."

"What he can't tell you, he may be able to tell your mother because of her position," Aunt Gwennie said.

"I swear, I feel like I'm back in the military."

"What do you mean?" Ami asked.

"Figuring out how to bend the rules in the military without breaking them? It's kind of a hobby," I explained. "Everybody does it. The military has some of the most ridiculous rules. Many of them prevent you from doing your job easily. We spend a lot of time figuring out which rules are important and which rules are just stupid and then finding ways to twist the stupid ones into pretzels. Hence, we find a way to do what we need to do without breaking them."

"Oh, yeah, we do that, too," Ami said with a nod.

My mother stared at her

Ami smiled in response. "So what do you want me to do, Mom?"

"You'll go with Astra to investigate the vandalism," Mom said.

"I'm sorry, you want me to take my younger sister on a police investigation?" Before she could answer, I shook my head no. "There's no way. I can't do that."

"You can't take Emma with you. She's in absolutely no condition to conduct an investigation, even one as simple as vandalism. You also have no idea if there are other effects on her judgment."

"Well, I'll go alone, then," I shrugged.

"You will not. We don't know if whatever is happening to them could affect witches, and you've already placed yourself in the middle of this pixie thing." Mom pointed toward Emma's phone. "That property you have to investigate is right near the pixie territory."

"You don't know that." I frowned and unlocked the phone.

"I do."

Tapping the police software, I read the encrypted message from the chief. Mom was right. The vandalized property the chief called about was right next to the swamp we were in earlier today. The swamp Pistachio Waterflash reigns over like a seven-inch green-haired Don Juan. "How did you know that?" I asked, looking up. "How did you know where the property was?"

"I am the high priestess of this coven. I know you don't think much of that role sometimes, but it does confer on me certain unexpected moments of epiphany." She smiled with smug delight as she straightened her shoulders, and then her face fell. "All moments of grandstanding aside, Astra—the pixies can be dangerous foes if they've been corrupted or angered in some way. I don't want you going out alone."

"You do realize when I was in the military, I would chase murderous pixies across continents all by myself?" I appreciated her consideration for my safety, but it was Ami's safety I was concerned with. She couldn't even drink legally. I found it hard to believe that she would know how to handle five pixies hell-bent on attacking. "I have plenty of tools from the Ministry in my Jeep. I'll be fine."

"My Jeep," Aunt Gwennie corrected. "And if you want to take my Jeep to the property, I agree with your mother. You need to take Ami with you."

"I can just take Emma's Malibu," I shrugged.

"Why are you so stubborn?" my mother asked with exasperation.

"Because Ami doesn't know how to fight. What can she do if confronted by a rabid pixie? Fling the death card at them and hope for a really vicious paper cut?"

I glanced at Ami, hoping I didn't offend her too much, but she didn't look offended. She looked like she agreed with me.

"I know how to fight," Althea murmured. "I can fling any number of potions at someone, and I guarantee the effects are far more than a paper cut." She turned toward my mother. "Astra's right. Ami might be older, but if you don't want her to go alone, I'm probably the best prepared to defend myself or to defend her."

"Look, I don't need defending," I told my younger sister.

"I didn't say you needed defending. I just said I was capable of it if the situation called for it." Althea stared at my mother, her face inscrutable. "The sun is setting. Make your determination quickly. I need a few moments to gather what I need if I am to go." Althea waited with a straight face, her hands clasped in front of her.

Ami nodded. "Mom, she's right. I'd like to sit here and brag that I'm all tough and could handle myself in a fight, but that's not true. I'm soft and squishy. Althea's like a walking, talking female version of Professor Snape from Harry Potter," Ami joked. "She's unflappable."

"Don't sell yourself short; you were pretty good at Parrot Paradise," I told Ami.

"I was not."

"Of course you were. You didn't run."

"But I didn't fight," she responded. "I think that's the point."

"You didn't need to."

"And if I had needed to, I wouldn't have." Ami looked at Althea. "Thea would've slammed bottles of burning acid in their faces before they got within three feet of her."

Althea half-smiled. "Maybe not acid."

ALTHEA'S SATCHEL of warlike potions clinked at her feet each time the Jeep hit a bump. The fourth time it shifted with a chime-like jingle, I asked, "Are you sure they won't break? The Jeep's a rough ride—and if we have to go over dirt, it's not going to get any smoother."

"They won't break," Althea assured me. "The bottles are enchanted to be extra strong. I came up with the spell after Ayla broke one too many of my really valuable potions." She sighed. "I wasn't able to re-create a few of them, either."

I nodded. "Good deal. Well, not that Ayla dropped your potion."

"Potions. Plural." Althea shifted in the seat.

"She's nosy, that one."

"But how are they going to break when you throw them at someone if they're enchanted not to break? I mean, I assume they're meant to be thrown at someone."

"Or on the ground, yes. They're each enchanted—the bottles—to disintegrate when flung at a certain velocity toward their target," she responded evenly. "The ones meant for offense or defense toward beings will disintegrate when hitting flesh. Obfuscation potions, area of effect potions? Those break when hitting the ground at a certain angle."

"So they don't break when dropped," I guessed.

"You got it."

Each of my sisters' personalities was coming into focus for me. Ami was quiet, knowledgeable, and insightful—the picture of an empathic seer whose purpose in life was to bring emotional balance to people. Ayla, at just thirteen, was a rambunctious kid whose mouth often bit off more than she could chew. But even that made sense with her powers—translocation and the ability to speak to the dead.

Mom claimed Althea, though, was a healer. I glanced over toward my fifteen-year-old sister, bottles of battle between her feet, and wondered if Mom was right in her assessment of Thea's nature. There was a sense of quiet menace in her that didn't fit the idea in my head of a healer. A steely determination that didn't fit. She caught me glancing at her.

"What?"

"The bottles." I jerked my chin toward her stash. "I'm just confused. I thought Mom said you were a healer?"

"I am a healer," she answered simply.

"Okay, why does a healer have a bunch of offensive potions, then?"

She was silent for a moment staring out the window. Then she nodded slightly and looked back at me. "I know mother calls me a healer, but what I really am is a potion master. Potions are my special talent. Healing potions, offensive potions, cursing potions. I have an instinctive understanding of how to put herbs and magics together in a bottle to create something...unique." Althea smiled at me. "And usually amazing, if I do say so myself."

"Useful talent to have."

"It is. But that talent includes healing potions, it includes poisons, and it also includes explosives. You can make almost anything into a potion if you know what you're doing," Althea explained. "The poisons and explosives Mom's not too impressed with. I'm fifteen years old, so mom calls me a healer because that's what she wants to see me do with my talent. That's the path she wants me to take. Heal people."

"That's not what you want to do?"

Althea paused a moment, thinking about it, and shrugged. "Not sure. I do want to heal people, but it's not the only thing I want to do. What I know is I can do many things. I'm not one thing. So I don't want to just be one thing. Mom disagrees, I guess."

"Understandable." I saw nowhere to go with that, so I let it pass without the comments I wanted to make to her. I struggled more and more to walk the fine line between my sisters and my mother's authority. I didn't want to challenge Mom's parental right to raise Ami, Althea, and Ayla in whatever way she wanted.

But I didn't want my sisters to become so frustrated with the limitations she forced onto them they would wind up like me—out the door and out of Mom's life.

Althea and I were quiet rolling through the sun-dappled streets of Forkbridge, both of us lost in thought about the future.

CHAPTER NINE

*T*he construction site was framed on one side by a major road that led in a straight shot to the highway but on three others? Pistachio Waterflash's swamp.

Pixie territory.

I parked the Jeep along the main road and looked toward the scraped and cleared patch of earth that would bring civilization to this previously natural area. Forkbridge, small though it was, needed to expand with the more significant population. The only place to go was out into the undeveloped area. In Florida, those areas belonged to the abundant wildlife.

Until they didn't.

The construction site was quiet, huge earth-moving machines still, but a few workers here and there stood talking. I checked my watch and wondered why they were still there. It was well past work hours.

"Hey, who is that?" Althea asked.

I looked up to find my sister pointing toward a woman standing tall at the center of the scraped earth patch. With a scowl, she stared around, intently examining all aspects of the construction site, while a man stood beside her. He was dressed like he could be the foreman. "She's too dressed up to work at a construction site."

Suddenly, she turned toward me, and I caught her entire face.

"Oh, it can't be," I breathed, recognizing her instantly. "I'm pretty sure that's Meryl Hawkins. What on earth is she doing here?"

"The reporter?" Althea craned her neck.

"Just met her this morning when she interviewed Emma and me."

"How'd that go?"

"Let's just say not as I'd planned and leave it at that."

Althea turned and raised an eyebrow.

"She wanted me to do psychic parlor tricks, handed me a pen to read. Well, I read it all right. Unfortunately, someone she had an affair with gave it to her." My sister rolled her eyes and chuckled softly. "I know, right? They never learn."

Althea glanced around the quiet site again. "I don't see any vandalism. Do you?"

"Much to my eternal disappointment, we have to get out of the car to investigate. But no, offhand, I don't see anything spray-painted or lit on fire or destroyed." I scanned the area looking for anything that didn't belong, but other than Meryl Hawkins? Nothing jumped out at me.

The lights had come on as night approached, but their brightness only partially dispelled the gloom of this isolated area. Blinding illumination and dark shadow alternated, exposing and hiding the damage done in the name of progress (and the mechanical tools used to do it).

I know. I sound like a crazy tree hugger, right?

I'm not a fervent environmentalist, mind you —though, to some extent, all witches are born that way. We connect to nature, have a profound affinity for it. Paranormals, in general, always had a solid bond to the natural world. It's built into who we are in a way it doesn't seem to be in humans. At least not in a way you guys seem aware of.

Well, okay, some of you are.

Anyway, I'm getting off track.

Even though I'm not a tree hugger, it's still difficult for me to see what was once natural, beautiful, and the home to so much flora and fauna scraped flat for a Punktex grocery store. Which, since Paul Wakefield was involved, is what I assumed this location would be.

"What do you want me to do?" Althea asked me.

"Well, I need to talk to those people over there." I pointed. "And I may not have the power of prophecy like Ami, but I'm going to bet Meryl Hawkins is going to have a lot of questions regarding why we're here." I leveled my gaze at Althea. "So, I'm not going to tell you what to do, but here's what you shouldn't do. No matter what, never say anything in front of a reporter. Don't give her anything to put in an article. Don't give her any information. Nothing. If you can help it, don't even speak when she's within earshot."

"I can do that," Althea said. "I'm the quiet sister, remember?"

Quiet like a creeping panther trying to sneak up on a gazelle, maybe.

If someone asked me to line my sisters up from most exuberant to least exuberant, Ayla would be first in line, followed by Ami and then

Althea. Ayla was all fire and excitement. Ami could get excited about something now and again, but for the most part, she held the center and was middle-of-the-road—and I don't mean that in a bad way. Stable, balanced people are few and far between.

Don't believe me? Think about it.

Althea was quiet, that was true—but there was a steady readiness to her. She watched things and people quietly, only speaking when she had something definitive to say. When I first returned home, I made a hasty judgment she was just shy.

Now I suspected she moved through life like a snake. Ready to strike if needed, conserving energy and movement if there was no reason to expend it.

Althea reached down into her bag and grabbed two bottles in each hand. Four colors of liquid sloshed around as she slipped each bottle into a separate pocket. Seconds later, I couldn't even see where she hid them.

"Did you make that tunic especially for something like this?" I asked her, surprised.

"I can sew, too." She tucked a strand of her raven black hair back into place. "You're not the only one with a magic outfit, you know. I could fit twenty of these in here, and you'd never hear so much as a clink until I went to grab one. And you'd only hear that because I forgot to take off my ring."

"I can't sew. This is military issue. How did you get a magic outfit?" I asked with a half-smile. "The seamstresses at the ministry were rare—and prized."

"Not a seamstress, though I can sew easy stuff. I'm a potion master, remember? Magic laundry detergent," Althea answered and then reached for the door.

"Well, if it isn't the police department's very own pet psychic," Meryl Hawkins said acidly upon seeing me. "What are you doing here?"

"Nice to see you again, Ms. Hawkins. I hope the day treated you well." My tone was mild, and I didn't bother to ramp up a temper at her snotty greeting, but I didn't go out of my way to de-escalate her snit fit, either.

Someone that started ramped up needed no help getting higher, and amped-up people say things they're trying to hide. I like amped-up people as long as they didn't pull a gun. They were useful. Since that was the case with Meryl, I quickly decided to simply give the reporter enough runway to crash into me all on her own.

This approach must've thrown her off because her expression darkened with contempt.

"I suppose you're here to talk to Gerald about the sabotage?" she asked.

"I got a call there was some vandalism on this job site. Emma's busy with another case, but she wanted me to come out here and get an initial report." I turned toward what I suspected was the construction foreman. "My name is Astra Arden. And you are?"

"Gerald Granger, ma'am," he said politely. Mr. Granger stuck his rough, calloused hand out to shake. "My son has actually told me all about you. It's an honor to meet you, Miss Arden."

"Your son?" I mentally raced through the people I knew in Forkbridge—which, to be honest, wasn't a long list yet. Suddenly, it clicked. "You must be Officer Adam Granger's father." He nodded happily. "I'm surprised I didn't recognize you. The two of you look so much alike you're practically twins." He gave me a look that said he didn't believe me but appreciated the statement.

Gerald Granger had nearly a hundred pounds on his son and the rough, grizzled look of someone who'd done physical labor all his life. In the shadows of his burly face, though, I could see the handsome young man he'd once been. "Adam said you were a smart one," Mr. Granger told me.

"Well, let's hope I'm smart enough to get this investigation started while Emma is otherwise occupied." I tilted my head and raised an eyebrow. "The call was for vandalism, but Ms. Hawkins here said sabotage. Since reporters never engage in hyperbole, I have to ask—is the report I got wrong? What happened?"

Yes, I delivered the statement in a tone just as smooth and silky as a cup of fresh cream. And yes, the crack about reporters and hyperbole caused Meryl Hawkins to turn at least three shades of red.

Maybe four.

"Gerald here said the machines have had parts stolen out of them—" Meryl started angrily but stopped when I swiftly held up my hand.

"Ms. Hawkins, you're aware that I need to get the information directly from the parties involved and not from the press, correct?" I made the statement sound as friendly and unassuming as possible. Even so, she gave me a look in return that would have melted lead in three seconds. "I'm sure you're just excited about the information that you've already gotten, and I can absolutely appreciate that."

"Can you now?" the reporter responded with a forced smile.

"But I do need the person in charge of the site to let me know what happened here, all right?"

"That might be true if you're a police officer, but you're not a police officer."

"No, she's a psychic. My son Adam says she's an incredible psychic, too," Mr. Granger told Meryl excitedly. "Closed all these cold cases the regular police could never figure out without her help. Did you hear about that, Ms. Hawkins? The police department must really be taking this seriously if they sent their only psychic out here to check out our complaint!" Gerald Granger turned and smiled widely. "This is the most exciting thing that's happened to me in years!"

Bless his heart, as my Aunt Gwennie would say. This man was so good-natured he could sense none of the hostility bubbling all around him.

"What she does is completely unethical!" Hawkins exploded.

The foreman stared at Meryl Hawkins and looked confused.

I heard Althea's bottles clink softly.

Oh, goodness.

I flashed my palm briefly toward her, and the sound of glass ceased.

The last thing I needed with Emma acting like a lovesick crazy person was having to explain to the chief why my fifteen-year-old sister put the uppity reporter in a coma with a bottle.

I took a deep breath. "I can understand why some people feel that way. Especially about telepaths. They can simply pluck an idea right out of your head as you're walking by." I slowly rolled down my gloves. Meryl's eyes grew wide as she watched the slow exposure of my arm. "I, though, can't do that. To get what I get, I have to touch an item or a person. So, you know, there's not really a lot of ethical play in what I do."

One glove off.

Meryl chewed her lower lip nervously.

"If I touch somebody without them wanting to be touched, that would be assault by contact. Did you know that?" I asked the reporter. "Florida is actually pretty tough regarding its assault charges. You can just threaten someone with a knife, and even if you didn't touch them?" Second glove off. "It's still assault. I've been learning so much since I been working with Emma." I handed my gloves to Althea and turned back to Meryl. "It really has been absolutely fascinating."

Gerald Granger, still oblivious to the tension, nodded happily. "Adam told me that very same thing! You really gotta wonder why there needed to be a 'me, too' movement if you could just throw a guy in jail for putting his finger on you, and you didn't want him to have it there."

"Because no man would prosecute another man for doing something like that to a woman," Althea interjected quietly. "Just because the laws were on the books didn't mean they protected anybody. Least of all women."

"Are we about to break out in a protest?" the reporter sneered.

"Oh, I'm sorry, I got distracted." I extended my un-gloved hand toward her, ignoring her comment. "In any case, Ms. Hawkins, I really am sorry if I rubbed you the wrong way somehow." I stared into her eyes, my expression extending a challenge my voice didn't even hint at. "How about we let bygones be bygones and start over?" The reporter broke our locked gaze to look at my bare, pale extended hand. "Perhaps we can help each other on this case. Deal?"

Of course, she didn't take it.

And with that confrontational handshake

reaching for her, she quickly turned and stormed back toward the street.

I tried not to laugh as I put my gloves back on.

"THAT YOUNG LADY certainly is a bit ill-tempered," Mr. Granger told me cheerfully. It made me wonder if he really was oblivious or just chose to ignore her outbursts.

Either way, I'd spent only moments with the older man, but I already liked him. With his happy-go-lucky personality and upbeat charm, he was a light and refreshing contrast to Pistachio Waterflash, probable sleazeball. Give me a cheerful construction worker over a seven-inch wanna-be Lothario—or a snotty reporter with a chip on her shoulder, come to think of it —any day.

I nodded. "I don't know her very well, but it certainly seems so. If you don't mind me asking, how did she wind up here before the police? I just got the phone call less than an hour ago from the chief, and it sounded like he had just gotten the report himself."

"Well, I don't right know, Miss Arden," he

answered, again using that old-fashioned Southern way of addressing unmarried women.

Years ago, I probably would've gotten annoyed by it, but it seemed endearing coming from Gerald. And at least he didn't call me Miss Astra.

"What time did she show up here?" I asked Gerald. "How soon was it after you called the police station to report what happened, do you think?"

"It was right quick, ma'am. Let's see." Gerald rubbed his scraggly five o'clock shadow and looked off toward the sky. "It was only about ten minutes after I called. And I called the police at"—Gerald looked at his cell phone—"6:32. So she must've been here at about quarter to seven?" He turned toward two men chatting about five feet behind him. "Joe Bob, that reporter woman showed up just before seven, yeah?"

Joe Bob stopped his in-depth talk about the Tampa Bay Buccaneers and turned. "I wasn't paying all that much attention, but you can check the gate camera." He pointed toward a temporary building just north of where we were standing. "That should have timestamps, and it catches everything coming or going."

"You want to see that?" Gerald asked.

I nodded.

"Right now?"

"In just a second, Mr. Granger. Can you explain to me exactly why you called the police? The chief said vandalism; the reporter said sabotage first and then theft second. So, can you explain to me exactly what's happening?"

"Well, sure I can—wouldn't it be more fun, though, if you just walked around the job site and touched things and tried to guess?" The foreman looked at me eagerly. I could tell he was fighting hard to keep the excitement out of his voice.

"No," I answered. "That would not be more fun. First, I don't guess; I read objects. And second, that would take a lot more time." And energy. "It's much easier if you simply tell me what happened."

"Oh." His face fell. "It just sure would've been cool to see a psychic work. Yep. That sure would've been a thing to tell the grandkids." He sighed. I waited. He sighed again.

"Mr. Granger?"

"Yes, Miss Arden?"

"Are you going to tell me what happened?"

"Oh, right, right, I just...Like I said, seeing a psychic at work, that would've been mighty exciting. Yes, mighty exciting." Mr. Granger nodded.

"I can understand that, sir."

He paused again and looked at me expectantly.

After about thirty seconds, Gerald seemed to realize I would not run around fondling his construction site for funzies. He finally answered.

"What happened wasn't all that involved. At five o'clock we took a break to have some coffee. Shoot the breeze, check in with what had been done. You know. Take stock of where we were before we left for the day."

Ah, yes, the creative practice of having casual meetings just when overtime kicked in. I was familiar with the concept.

"Well, an hour later, we went back to store all the equipment, and nothing would start. The graders wouldn't start, the bulldozers wouldn't start, the excavators wouldn't start. Turn the key and nothing." Mr. Granger mimicked turning a key and made clicking sounds. "Now, Joe over there is a pretty good mechanic, but when he looked to find out what was going on?"

"The fuel injectors were all missing," Joe Bob said loudly.

"The fuel injectors were all...missing?" I asked, frowning. "On everything?"

"Yep. Digger? No fuel injectors. Excavator? No fuel injectors. I checked every machine that wouldn't move," Joe Bob said, his voice still echoing with surprise. "Those fuel injectors are not exactly easy to remove. How someone got 'em all out in just one hour, I'll never know."

"Could it have been a group of people working together, then?" I asked.

Mr. Granger shook his head no. "We were standing right over there. We would've seen them. You couldn't have ten people running around on this job site removing fuel injectors with no one seeing them and the camera not catching them."

"Yeah, we could all see the whole place," Joe agreed. The man next to him agreed with his two coworkers.

"No full-size man could have walked through here without being seen, much less the number needed to remove all those injectors that quick."

"Well. No, not a full-size man," I said under my breath.

CHAPTER TEN

"There." Althea kept her voice low. Glancing behind her to ensure Gerald and Joe were on the other side of the office, she pointed to a small spot on the screen. "I know it's hard to see, but something is moving on the ground. And it's not moving like an animal would move. It's deliberate, straight. It's gotta be a pixie."

I squinted.

Her younger eyes must work slightly better than mine. I took a few seconds and several replays of the security tape to spot what she caught instantly.

"You see it now?"

"You're talking about that, right?" I pointed to the grainy image in the corner of the screen, dragged my finger in a line across toward the bulldozer, and then tapped again where the tiny thing disappeared. "The thing that just ran from there to there?"

"Yep. It's gotta be a pixie," Althea breathed.

With the low-end black and white recording, there was no way to tell for sure whether it was a pixie or not. Had the video been in color, it would have been easy to identify the shock of bright red hair.

As it stood, we could barely identify the moving shadow as a pixie, much less which pixie. If it was a pixie. Which I wasn't sure of.

"It could be. But why would they disable all the engines?" I looked out the window and stared into the trees surrounding the site. "And why fuel injectors? Fuel injectors for these aren't exactly difficult to get. Gerald will have them up and running as soon as the mechanic gets the parts." I looked at my sister. "At the most, they delayed construction for a day. Maybe two."

Althea bit her lip and pondered potential reasons. "Someone was just trying to make a point?" It was a good guess. An excellent guess for a fifteen-year-old. "You know, just to get their attention?"

"Okay, that's an idea, but take it further. What point? And to who?"

My sister's face twisted as she racked her brain for some simple solution to the mystery of the missing fuel injectors. Still, a few minutes later, she shrugged. "I don't think we have enough information. Do you?"

No, I didn't think we had enough information.

It still felt like I was missing something.

It was far too incredible a coincidence the owner of Punktex followed Pistachio the pixie—and also was the wealthy owner of the grocery store being built. That much I was sure of. Add in Emma's magical bewitchment the moment we came face-to-face with Pistachio Waterflash?

It was just too coincidental.

But why would the pixies sabotage construction machines? If Alice Windrow is mesmerized by Pistachio Waterflash, why wouldn't he just ask her not to build the store here? From what I saw, she wouldn't refuse him anything he asked of her. There was no reason I could see for the pixies to sneak onto Alice's construction site to damage their machines.

"Something's not adding up here," I told Althea. "The thing I can't get past is those machines are not crippled. Any mechanic could come in with the right parts and get everything back and running within, what…six hours, maybe?" I raised my eyebrow. "So why do it? Why cause such a temporary shut down?"

Althea shrugged. "The pixies must know something we don't."

"Great call, Captain Obvious. Clearly, they know something we don't. The question is what. What is their true agenda here?"

She leaned closer and dropped her voice almost to a whisper. "You mean more than just Pistachio, then, I guess?"

"No." I stopped and looked up at her. "Wait. Why, what do you mean?"

"Well, you keep saying they and not him. That 'the pixies' must have an agenda, or 'the pixies' know something we don't. That implies to me you talked to more than just one pixie, but you didn't say you did," Althea pointed out. "If you only met Pistachio Waterflash, then you only know how he feels and what he thinks." My sister tilted her head. "The rest of the pixies may not agree with him at all."

I scratched my chin and thought about it. Pixie clans were notoriously close-knit. Until they weren't. "Fair point, but he is their chieftain. I think it's safe to assume they'd follow his lead whether they disagree with him or not."

"And when the Witches' Council was ruling Imperatorial City, all of you folks in the military totally agreed with everything they did all the time? No one ever planned a coup to unseat them and totally change the paranormal government?" Althea's sardonic expression belonged to a woman much older than fifteen years. "You're assuming his leadership is secure, and the other pixies support him in what he's doing. That's a pretty big assumption, Astra."

"It is," I agreed. "You think that's a mistake? Even knowing what we know about pixie clans?"

"I just think you need to stop thinking of them as a group. He's one dude. If you have no evidence the other pixies agree with him or support what he's doing, don't assume. Unless you have evidence to the contrary." My sister crossed her arms. "Which I don't think you do. And we do have evidence that Archie is really upset with Pistachio for some reason. Not the pixies. Pistachio." Althea stepped back. "There might be a lot more going on here with them than we realize. That's all I'm saying."

When I first returned to Forkbridge, I was concerned my personality would make reintegration into my family difficult. I assumed my mother had raised three flighty, hippie, roses-and-incense witches who wouldn't know common sense if it sparked out of a cauldron and spoke to them.

What I found were sisters far more similar to me than I ever would've expected.

"You up for traipsing through the wilds of south Forkbridge?" I asked her.

Althea nodded.

"Okay, let me get Gerald a police report so insurance will cover the replacement of the fuel injectors," I told her. "Then we'll go looking for the pixie—or pixies—that stole them."

THE SUN HAD SUNK below the horizon by the time we investigated the area around the Punktex construction site. Nearly at the undeveloped terrain, Althea reached into her shirt and pulled out a small zippered carrier that held dozens of tiny vials. Just a drop of "Cat's Eye" on my tongue, and the dark black shadows lifted into a washed-out gray. It meant we could investigate the dark marshland now, but it also meant we were somewhat nearsighted. Fine detail was just a memory.

Not the most fantastic thing when you're searching for people no bigger than seven inches.

"I didn't know you could write police reports," Althea said as we made our way deeper into the quagmire. I didn't know if Althea had ever had the pleasure of clambering through the muddy marshes of Central Florida, but I suspected not. Her face remained impassive, but every so often, she let out an unhappy squeak.

"I can write them. I'm not supposed to sign them."

"Oh? So why did you do it this time?"

"I faked Emma's signature," I told my sister, scanning the grass and sedges growing in clumps around the warm water. "Hopefully, she won't be mad at me when she comes out of whatever ecstasy stupor she seems to be stuck in."

"Right."

The wind rustled the grass, though we could barely hear it through the swarms of insects humming and buzzing. "I wish Archie wasn't having a snit fit. We could really use him. Even with your Cat's Eye potion, it's not easy to make things out in here."

"What do you think is going on with him?"

Althea asked, dodging a giant dragonfly. "I mean, I know he's got an attitude and everything, but dive-bombing the pixie chieftain seems out of character even for him." The dragonfly paid absolutely no mind as he zipped past her.

"If pixies taste like a rabbit, maybe not so out of character."

"You didn't answer my question."

"Because I don't have an answer. Hopefully, Mom will figure it out, or he'll be able to tell her. What made you think the pixies might be going rogue?"

"I read a book once that said fey people never quite do what you tell them to do or quite what you think they will."

Althea's voice was uncommonly calm for a fifteen-year-old clambering through the dark in a pixie-controlled swamp. I was beginning to understand Ami's comment that she was unflappable. She had the delivery of a sixty-year-old professor that had long passed the time when he was shocked or surprised by anything.

"Profound," I told her. "What book?"

"I forget what it was in. But for some reason, that line stuck with me." She glanced back at me. "I also read that pixies are usually ruled by women, not men. So the male chieftain seems curious."

"That's true," I agreed. "The men are usually subservient to the women. Like most fey folk, they have a form of equality, though. At least, as far as we were educated back in the ministry. Leadership positions? You're right." I slapped a mosquito on my neck. "Almost always held by women."

"From what you told me about Pistachio Waterflash, I don't really see how someone with the personality to do what he's doing could get elected chieftain."

"I didn't really describe much, Althea. What makes you say that?"

She stopped and turned back to face me. "It's obvious that whatever's been done to Emma was not done with her consent. The pixies may enjoy playing jokes and manipulating people, but they almost always do so with some level of consent. If Emma didn't give her consent—and we know she did not because you were there—why are we assuming Alice gave her consent?" Before I could answer, Althea continued. "I don't need to know much more about him than that. He manipulates women without their consent. There's really nothing more that can be said about such a creature."

I considered her guileless expression and marveled at how well it matched her matter-of-fact tone. "Like you said before, though, we don't know that for sure. We don't know what Alice agreed to and what she didn't. All we know is what she told us."

"We know that Emma was manipulated without her consent, so nothing she's said can be relied upon as truth," Althea said with a steely glint in her eye. "That tells me as much about Pistachio Waterflash as I need to know to justify my mistrust."

I REALIZED while traipsing through the mud that Archie and the star power might have come to me because the paranormal world was a growing threat to humans. That made solving these cases far more complicated—first, I had to narrow down whether the danger was supernatural or human, and then I had to neutralize the threat.

Which, if paranormal, could get...complicated.

Before the coup, as Althea called it, the

paranormal world had strict rules for interacting with the human one.

As in, we didn't. At all. Ever.

Okay, we weren't supposed to.

Most paranormals lived in paranormal towns shielded from the human world. The few paranormals residing in the human world abided by a strict code. It kept all paranormals, including themselves, hidden from the humans.

Again, they were supposed to. Violations of the code resulted in arrest and possible execution —and yes, that was abused by the Witches' Council more than I'd like to admit. There were reasons behind it, and I can't say I disagreed with the rule (even if I disagreed with the consequences of violating it).

But that all changed with the new regime. The rule was tossed out in the name of freedom of choice. It was now advised that we remain hidden —but not required.

Some of us ran out of the sparkly closet and let our freak flag fly.

Most paranormals, though, understood the wisdom of keeping ourselves hidden from view. The threat of death from our own rules may have gone away, but the danger of persecution from the humans kept most of us quiet about what we are.

"Why are you in our territory, witch?" a small, tinny voice from the dark interrupted my thoughts with as brutal a directness as one could manage, while still sounding like a dog's squeaky toy. "No one has given you permission to come here."

I scanned the area near my feet, but the lack of fine detail prevented my recognition of my feet, much less anything actually standing near me on the ground. I couldn't see the pixie confronting me.

"Why are you here?" the voice asked again, and I froze. Now it was a rich and loud woman's voice, and the timbre of a threat was unmistakable.

This pixie wasn't at my feet.

They were at least my size, if not larger.

"Get behind me," I told Althea, dragging her back. "And keep your hands out of your pockets for the moment." Standing taller, I called out, "Show yourself, pixie."

"How dare you give me commands in my own swamp," the pixie responded brusquely. "I am Amethyst Cloudspirit, guardian of this place and fierce warrior of the Waterflash clan."

"Good for you," I responded. "My name is—"

"I didn't ask you what your name was," she hissed. "I know who you are, Astra of the Arden clan. We have known of your coven since we came to this place. We have left one another alone until now." I scanned the trees but could see nothing. "I asked you what you are doing here, and I expect an answer."

As if magician's smoke cleared to reveal the trick, Althea and I were suddenly surrounded by six full-sized red-tunicked female pixies. It was like they appeared fully formed from the flora itself—rising up from ditches, out of leaves, and emerging with a splash from shallow pools of water. They all gripped large staffs firmly in their hands. "Althea, I can't see their expressions very well," I whispered. "I need to."

My sister quickly handed me a tiny vial. "One drop."

I tapped it on my tongue and nearly choked on the strong flavor of cinnamon. Within seconds, my vision darkened but cleared.

"You're trying my patience, witch."

I scanned quickly over the six ladies and focused on a purple-haired woman with a bearing that telegraphed she was in charge. I raised my left hand and gestured toward her. "You're Amethyst Cloudspirit?"

In response, Cloudspirit dropped into an attack stance and raised her staff. "Put your hands down, witch, and answer my question. Your defiance is brave, but I promise you, it won't get you anywhere."

"I thought pixies were cheerful?" Althea whispered. Her voice was steady. I'd worried she would be frightened, but there was no outward sign of it if she was. "These are pixies, right? Even though they're big?"

"We are cheerful when we have cause to be, and we are vengeful when we have cause to be," Amethyst responded with a sneer at my sister. "Right now, we have no cause to be cheerful. Witches are invading our territory, and our—" The angry pixie abruptly stopped as if she'd said too much and eyed the two of us suspiciously. "Answer my question! Do not distract me!" Her face reddened.

With an irritated sigh, I nodded. "You know what? I don't see any point in hiding why we're here. Someone sabotaged all the construction machines at the site on the northeast end of this marsh. There's no way a human could have done it, but a pixie could've crawled right up in there and stolen the fuel injectors."

"We didn't steal anything!" a neon green-haired pixie to the right of Amethyst burst out indignantly. "Pixies don't steal, witch!"

"Ebony, shut up," Amethyst told her.

"Ebony?" I asked, surprised. "Are you the same Ebony that told Pistachio Waterflash I would be coming?" Ebony's eyes widened as my own narrowed.

Pistachio had known somehow Emma was coming as well, and now Emma was *non compos mentis*. Was this troll-haired pixie the reason he had time to prepare his attack? The anger rose with the bile in my esophagus.

"We're not here to answer your questions, witch," Amethyst spat while placing a hand on Ebony's shoulder. "Tread lightly. Only pixies may ask questions of our seer."

"Tread lightly?" I asked with enough disdain to get my point across.

"Tread lightly," she answered with enough menace to get her point across.

Okay, that's it.

"Your seer told your chieftain that my friend was coming with me into 'your' territory, and now my friend is acting like a lunatic," I spat back, the first outward sign of the temper rising in the back of my throat. "I get you're all defensive about incursions into your stinky swamp, but I'm defensive about my friend's mind being toyed with. If you people hadn't attacked first—twice—we wouldn't even be here. So maybe you need to answer my questions."

"Careful, witch. You're outnumbered," Amethyst warned me coldly. Her finger tapped against the bamboo staff.

"You have no idea how fast that can change," I responded just as coldly, pulling myself up to full height. "Not that I'd need to. In case you know my name but not who I am? I trained in the Ministry of Arcane Fugitives, Cloudspirit. If you think I need to get other people to take on six pixies with twigs, then you've been out of the loop, friend."

Cloudspirit eyed me with predatory calculation. "We are not friends, witch."

I raised my eyebrow. "Okay, Rainbow Xena."

"Astra," Althea said quietly.

I glanced over my shoulder. "Stay behind me."

"Maybe it would be easier if we each answer the other's questions," she said in a reasonable tone. "Clearly, the pixies have questions for you, and you have questions for the pixies." Althea stepped out from behind me. "I think, in your defensive stance, you failed to notice something that I'm really curious about."

"What's that?" I asked.

"They have not called their chieftain," Althea pointed out. "Despite the incursion into their territory, Amethyst Cloudspirit is questioning you herself instead of taking you directly to the leader of their clan. None of these women have countered her choice to do so." Althea turned toward her and nodded respectfully. "I, for one, would like to know why that is."

CHAPTER ELEVEN

We followed the six pixie fighters deeper into the Florida jungle. They had a place, they assured us, we could speak freely without being overheard—even at full size. Who would overhear us—the alligators? Through the overgrown and untamed marsh, we traipsed silently along a faint path winding its way north.

"Are we almost there?" I asked impatiently. Ironic, since the pixies were known for their childlike demeanors, my sister was fifteen, and I was supposed to be the grown-up in the group. "It feels like we're walking to Miami."

"You seem anxious, Astra of Arden clan," one of the pixies responded. It was difficult to tell which one in the darkness, but I could sense she was to my right. "Ebony Cottonspring agreed to speak with you. That is an honor. Why would you still be on guard?"

"Because you're dragging my younger sister and me even further into this swampy quagmire. Just because your snippy leader agreed to talk doesn't mean you won't turn on us at any time and attack. This could all be a trick."

"Ebony is our seer, not leader. Is that what you think might happen? That we would give you assurances and then turn on you?" she asked, her voice indicating her surprise. "Do other witches answer honestly so infrequently that your first instinct is to not believe us when we make an agreement?"

Since when did pixies talk like they walked out of Rivendell after lunching with the elves in Middle Earth? They're supposed to be lighthearted and fun. This wasn't lighthearted or fun. If anyone pulled a ring out with elvish on it, I was out of here.

"I don't know you, pixie."

"Does anyone really know another being? Do we know ourselves?" she mused. "Socrates famously declared that the unexamined life was not worth living. Perhaps you are seeing your own subconscious desires mirrored in your fears about us."

Just my luck. I found the only pixies on the planet with a penchant for talking like elves and an interest in philosophy. Was nothing in Florida normal? Did everything—even the paranormals—have to be just a little weird? "Considering how we met, I think it's a pretty good idea for me to remain on alert. Don't you?"

"We don't know you, either," she responded.

"Even so, we are bringing you to our hiding place," another chimed in.

"Witches have so little trust," yet another added. "A paradox of their supposed empathy. Don't you agree?"

That they were leading us to their super-secret hideout in their swamp hadn't precisely been confirmed yet. "Let's just say I court optimism, but I'm not gonna be marrying it anytime soon."

"What an interesting way to put it," a pixie said from behind me.

I rolled my eyes.

"Are you all right?" Althea whispered.

"Fine. How are you doing? Are you okay?"

"I'm fine," Althea responded evenly.

We continued picking our way through the bug- and snake-infested swamp.

Or maybe it was a jungle.

I don't know; it seemed like a swamp. It smelled like a swamp.

Florida had the most pristine, gorgeous outdoor areas in the whole country—as long as you were on the coast. If you're inland? The masses of terrifying bugs buzzing past your face were enough to make you think about moving somewhere with dry weather.

I heard Iceland was mosquito-free.

Iceland sounded good.

"Wait," Althea whispered. "Do you see that? What's that?"

The jungle foliage parted to reveal a small pond (no doubt teeming with alligators). The moonlight glistened eerily off the still water. An island lay in shadows about a thousand feet in front of us.

"Get in," Amethyst Cloudspirit told me, pointing to a small boat.

It wasn't painted. Heck, the boat didn't even look like it'd been sealed, the natural wood color patchy and dry. Ten feet long with no motor and seemingly no way to propel it from here to that tiny island, it didn't look like it could hold one of us—much less eight.

I shook my head. "You must be kidding. That thing is going to sink as soon as I step in." I leaned forward slightly and glanced in. No seats. "Or I'll fall over into the pond and get eaten by an alligator."

"You must," Ebony told me.

"No way." To be fair, my ministry outfit would protect me from the worst of any alligator attack, but my shoulders and face were exposed, and that would hurt. Althea, meanwhile, was unprotected. "Not a chance."

"I assure you. You will be safe. You and your sister," Ebony, the pixie's seer, told me as she held out her hand. "We can help you if you can't get in on your own. The alligators won't attack you. They live here with the understanding that they cannot attack the two-legs."

I stared at her outstretched hand with an eyebrow raised.

"Unless we tell them to," Amethyst murmured.

I remained unmoved by their assurances.

Althea leaned in. "Astra, we need their help. Someone has to trust first."

The purple-haired pixie scowled. "We were the

ones to trust first, Althea of the Arden clan. We have brought you here to this sacred place. Or did you forget," Amethyst told her with a mocking bow. She laughed suddenly for no apparent reason. "No wonder Pistachio dismissed you as a concern to his plans. The world revolves around you, and you take no one else's motivations into consideration."

"I find it ridiculous that a pixie is calling me self-involved," I said pointedly.

"We are self-involved because we have to be, witch," Ebony told me with warm sincerity that seemed to come out of nowhere. Her skin, a dark umber, made her wide eyes striking in the lightless jungle as she looked at me. "No gods to protect us. We have only ourselves to rely on, ourselves and our leadership." She shifted, her eyes drifting down. "And our leadership is—"

"Not here," Amethyst told Ebony sharply.

I looked at the rickety boat again and sighed.

LAZY HEAT TRAILS drifted up from the small pool at the very center of the island. Undersized flames danced within teeny, low ledges carved from tall rock walls surrounding the water. It gave the small area an ethereal glow.

Well, small to us at this size. I could spy tiny homes tucked beneath arched rocks no higher than my ankles.

I walked toward the heated reservoir and peeked over. I could see the smooth rock bottom in the shallow, clear water. It shimmered, dazzlingly, with moonlight as if the pool was lined in reflective quartz. Every once in a while, a burble punctuated the silence.

"This is our spring. We call it, in your language, the moon pool," Ebony explained, her voice proud, as Althea and I stared. "Pistachio would never come to this island or within these walls. This pool is designated for women only. The leaves above cover it when the sun rises and reveal it only when the moon climbs the sky." She turned and smiled at it as if it was an old friend. "Please, as sisters, have a seat around her magic and be made welcome."

"Is it a healing spring?" Althea stared into the water with wide-eyed fascination. "Have you ever used the water in magic? Does it have magical properties? Healing properties? Mineral properties? Has sunlight ever touched it at all? Like, directly, I mean, because the moonlight really is sunlight just reflected."

Ebony smiled at Althea and her rapid-fire

questions, but Althea didn't notice. My sister was too busy examining every aspect of the pool with her eyes.

"It is lovely, isn't it?" Ebony sighed.

Suddenly, my sister looked up, her expression apologetic. "I'm sorry. I know we're here for a totally different reason, but that thing? That thing is absolutely amazing. It's like a cave pool only... um, not."

"It is, I suspect, why our ancestors chose this place. There will be time to answer your questions, little sister." Ebony gestured toward the other pixies. They moved into a circle around the bubbling hot spring at a slight movement of her hand. "I can see in your eyes you have a tie to elixirs of magic, yes?" Althea nodded excitedly. "I am not just a seer for the pixies. I have some talent in seeing—"

"Could you two maybe have your hot spring appreciation night another time?" I asked the pixie testily. "I have two people back in my house acting like they were doused with a love drug, and one of them could be dead within forty-eight hours. I'm not trying to be rude"—actually, I didn't care if I was rude or not—"but I don't have time for this."

"What two people?" Amethyst Cloudspirit

asked me sharply. "Talk, witch, before I drown you in that—"

"Sister, let us keep this a safe, civil place," Ebony told the pale warrioress sharply, her hand lightly resting on the pale woman's forearm. "It is the sacred moon well of women, and they are women even if they are not pixies. They deserve temporary sanctuary here by virtue of that." She paused. "Without threat."

Awesome.

Feminist, philosophical pixies with Tolkienesque speech patterns.

I sighed.

Bless your heart, Florida.

Amethyst's muscled body arched toward Ebony protectively. The two stared silently at one another, and I could practically feel the overly aggressive woman wrestling with her will and the temptation to defy the seer. Finally, the hostile pixie jerked her chin once in agreement and looked at me expectantly. "You were saying?"

"I wasn't, but the two people are Detective Emma Sullivan of the Forkbridge Police Department and Alice Windrow—who I think you already know."

"That means there are now four," Ebony murmured, frowning.

"Four what?" I asked.

"Oh, no." Amethyst stepped in front of Ebony, her staff leaning out toward us. "I asked the first question this evening, and I still haven't received an answer. Do not mistake the seer's hospitality and generosity for capitulation to your agenda. Before we go any further, I want to know what you are doing here. Why have you come here, and what do you want?"

Whatever smoothing over Ebony had tried to do since we set foot on this island, Amethyst was still coiled like a spring. Beneath her outward submission to the seer's request for a peaceful conclave, the purple pixie was just looking for a reason to pop. Amethyst Cloudspirit agreed to allow this conversation to take place. Sure. Still, I could feel she was ready for it to turn in a different direction at any moment.

She wasn't the only one.

The light from the pixie-sized fires around the bubbling pool allowed me vision enough to take in the six paranormals confronting us. (Though black light would've been just as effective considering their hair was a variety of neon shades that would spice up a laser tag game.)

The other four looked to Amethyst and Ebony

as the leaders and spoke little. I suspected none of the four would make a move without permission from one of them, and I quickly shifted my focus to the principal pixies.

Since we'd entered into this small enclosure without a ceiling, Ebony's demeanor had become almost worshipful. Even if the pixies didn't have gods to protect them, the seer's reverence for this hot spring seemed as fervent as any religious zealot's devotion. Her aversion to violence in this place, in my estimation, was genuine.

That left Amethyst Cloudspirit.

Her leadership over the other five women was clear but not quite as simple in this place. Amethyst, while still in charge, was deferring to the seer pixie.

As long as that dynamic held, we were safe.

At least until I set off the vibrantly purple-headed pixie.

I relaxed my stance and dropped my hands, making sure they were visible. "I was investigating the sabotage of construction equipment at the site on the edge of your territory—"

"In our territory," Amethyst corrected.

"Yes, well, you don't have a map showing what you think you control, so I'm doing the best I can," I told her with a friendly smile she didn't seem convinced was friendly. "I came with my sister because the callout was for Emma, not me —but she's in no condition to be seen out in public by anyone. We ran into your chieftain earlier today, and since then, she's—"

"Overly enamored with him?" Ebony asked.

"An ardent admirer of Pistachio Waterflash?" Amethyst added wryly.

"Acting like a lovesick crazy person whose brain flew the coop?" the pink-haired pixie chimed in.

The dusky orange-red glow of the tiny flames illuminated the pixies' features clearly. If I was looking for surprise at this revelation, I wouldn't find it. I crossed my arms. "I take it you all are familiar with this phenomenon?"

"It is still your turn, witch," Amethyst reminded me calmly. "Finish your story, and then we will decide if we will tell you ours."

My shoulders tightened. "That wasn't the agreement."

Amethyst's eyes narrowed. "This is our sacred well. We decide what the agreement is."

Oh, I don't think so.

"I just told you I know two human beings that have been cursed to have a crush on your smarmy chieftain, none of you look surprised, but you still won't answer my questions or tell me what the heck that's about?" I asked defiantly—in complete opposition to my original plan not to provoke Amethyst Cloudspirit.

"You need to answer their questions, Astra," Althea told me calmly. I turned and stared at my sister in surprise. I'd often heard the same note of determination in my mother's voice. Still, I'd never heard it duplicated so precisely by anyone else. "We are in their sacred space as guests. For that alone? As an apology for the intrusion?" She shrugged. "Tell them what they want to know."

I clenched my teeth and stared at the serious girl half my age giving me orders in the field. If some new recruit in my division had spoken to me this way back at the ministry? In front of someone we were interrogating? I would've had them cleaning bathroom floors with a toothbrush for a month.

A magic toothbrush.

That cleaned nothing.

"It's the only way, and you know it." Althea's green eyes were penetrating as she looked into mine. "We don't want to war with the pixies."

"The child is wise beyond her years," Amethyst commented with amusement.

A HALF AN HOUR LATER, Ebony nodded. "We had heard tell of your star card power, but did not believe it. I have never heard of such a thing. A goddess long thought to be dead, her power reincarnating in another. Gifted by another goddess." Her dark face was alight with interest. "Fascinating. Truly fascinating."

"Astraea was the daughter of the dusk and the dawn," Amethyst said. The other four pixies nodded in agreement. "It is powerful magic you hold," she added grudgingly.

"I don't know that I have any extra magic because of it," I shrugged. "So far, all it seems to have gotten me is a smart-mouthed owl and a job with the police department. Which, to be honest, is kinda cool."

"The owl or the job?" Althea asked with amusement.

"Both. Or either. Or neither, depending on the day. Anyway, that's the story." I leaned back on the rock and stretched. "I know a pixie sabotaged the site, but I don't know why. I know something's happened to Emma, and I don't know why. I know Alice Windrow's life is threatened by something, but I don't know what."

"Well, you don't seem to know much. The goddess Athena chose you for this job?" Amethyst's voice cracked like a whip. "She must have very few followers left if you are the best she could do."

"We can't all be seven inches tall and live in a swamp," I retorted.

"Are you planning on swimming back to land?" the pixie responded in a harsh, suspicious tone of voice.

The two of us leaned forward to stand up.

"Stop it, both of you," Ebony said sharply. "The witch has kept her commitment to us to tell us the story. As a seer, I tell you I sense that she is telling the truth and has told us all that she is aware is important." Ebony looked at Amethyst. "Despite our reputation, we are not children. I will not have a schoolyard brawl at the moon pool. Do not be vengeful to one who does not deserve it."

"We don't know that she doesn't." Amethyst's eyes were aflame with frustration.

"Until you know that she does, keep your commitments, warrioress."

I leaned toward Althea. "When you're a hammer, every problem you come up against looks like a nail."

Amethyst's head turned, and she glared at me.

My sister stared at me with disappointment. "You really can be aggravating, you know that, sis?" Her voice held the echo of my mother.

I winked.

"Astra of the Arden clan, I ask you not to deliberately provoke Amethyst." Ebony smiled kindly. "In times like these, she is easily provoked, and it is she who can best tell her story simply." The seer's face clouded. "It is difficult for me to separate the images I see in the pool from things that have happened. She can tell you what is. I can tell you what might be."

"As your sister suspected, we have broken with our chieftain," Amethyst began, her hands balling into fists. "Pistachio Waterflash has disgraced our clan. He forced water from the sun pool into pixie dust. He created...well, a monstrosity of magic designed to manipulate human women."

"He calls it sun dust," Ebony added. "We urged him, begged him, to leave the humans alone. To stay out of their affairs. But with the Witches' Council gone, he sees no one that may tell him no." Her face twisted with hatred. "I do not know what he wants with these women or why he has turned them into worshipful servants like a god of old. But it is an atrocity and an immoral twisting of what we are."

"There are four women he's done this to?" I asked.

Amethyst nodded. "If what you say is true, Emma is the fourth. We knew of Alice. She, I believe, was the first—an easy mark, since she was already a follower."

"And the other two?" Althea asked.

"We know of them, but we only know the identity of one," Amethyst told me.

Ebony nodded wearily. "Meryl Hawkins, a reporter with the—"

"*Forkbridge Gazette.* Yep," I sighed. "I'm familiar."

Althea and I stared at each other.

CHAPTER TWELVE

"That purple-haired pixie was just insufferable," I mumbled.

"I can see why you would feel that way about it," Althea responded.

I glanced over. "About what?"

She opened her mouth to say something more but then glanced back at me and snapped it shut.

"Come on, tell me what you mean." We were driving along Beacon Street back toward the house after finishing our confab with the rebel pixies. The evening didn't go how I'd planned, but we did get more information about the pixie drama than we'd had to start. That was a good thing. And I didn't get into a fistfight with

186 | LEANNE LEEDS

Amethyst Cloudspirit, so that was a win, too. "I mean, anyone would find her annoying."

"No, I don't think just anyone would find her annoying." I could feel my sister's eyes on me. "I think you found her annoying—but like I said, that's not surprising. I read somewhere that the people who annoy us the most often exhibit the things about ourselves—"

"Oh, hold on a minute. I'm nothing like that pixie," I told Althea hotly, shooting her a look of incredulity. "I'm the complete opposite of that woman."

My sister stared at me. "Yeah, okay."

"She's arrogant, and jumps to conclusions, and seems to deal with everything more aggressively than she needs to. She's got no patience. No subtlety. No finesse."

"Yeah, nothing like you, Blunty McBlurtness."

I stopped talking and gripped the steering wheel.

After a bit, Althea leaned down and emptied her pockets of unused potion bottles into the duffel bag at her feet. Once done, she clicked on the radio and turned it up. The Pixies "Where is My Mind" filled the Jeep.

Althea tapped her fingers with no sense of irony.

IT WAS LATE when we returned to Arden House.

"How are they?" I asked Ami, pointing toward the two women curled up on the couch asleep. "They're safe, at least." Emma snored loudly. "And still breathing."

"Physically safe, sure. But as far as getting their minds back? Well, let's just say Alice seems to be going further and further down the rabbit hole, and Emma's right there with her." Ami moved toward the back of the couch and looked down. "I did readings for them both trying to figure out what's going on, but I don't think the cards help with this. The Tower came up over and over again." Ami turned and rolled her eyes. "It's like, tell me something I don't know."

Althea gave Ami a sidelong glance. "I think we had better luck."

"Oh?"

"There is a war between the pixies. A group of female pixies is challenging Pistachio Waterflash and his right to rule—though I'm not sure he knows that yet. They claim that he's used their sun pool water and pixie dust to come up with some kind of Ecstasy-like drug."

"Ecstasy?" Ami's face showed her adorably innocent confusion.

"It's a psychoactive drug that produces altered sensations, increased energy, empathy, and makes people want to jump into bed with anyone that smiles at them." She shuddered. "Feels good, I guess, but it's nasty stuff. People take it at clubs, and it turns them into hippies that love everyone." Althea wrinkled her nose. "They can also dance for hours like coked-up Wall Street bros on a binge," Althea explained. "I only call it ecstasy-like because the sun dust appears to produce that overwhelming 'love everybody' effect, at least."

"How do you know anything about coked-up Wall Street bros?" I asked Althea, surprised. Ami acted like Rapunzel locked in a tower half the time, oblivious to the real world. I assumed Althea's experience of the world was similar.

My sister snorted with amusement. "I've seen every *Law & Order* ever made. Potions don't involve a huge amount of concentration once you've got it down, so I keep it on in the background. I've seen them all, some twice," she said. "And I mean every one of them. Including *SVU, Criminal Intent, LA—*"

"I get it, I get it," I said, holding my hands up. "I forget you guys have internet."

"Have it, use it. Well, some of us. In any case, the victims love everybody. In a drug or magic-induced sense."

"Except they don't love everybody, they just love Pistachio," I said.

"That makes sense, then, with what Mom found out here. Your owl is upset with Pistachio because he's trying to form his own religion." Ami frowned. "Or maybe has his own religion? I wasn't completely clear on the difference between trying to form one and having one, and to be honest, it sounds like nobody else is, either."

"Why didn't he just say that instead of trying to eat the pixie?"

"Since he's Athena's owl, he's not allowed to pass judgment on religious beliefs. Apparently, the gods all got together years and years ago. They made some agreement that they can't denigrate each other's beliefs." Ami held up her hands. "So he couldn't tell you."

"The gods are religiously tolerant?" I asked with a raised eyebrow. "I'm not trying to be lame-brained here, but are they aware of history? Like, in any capacity? If they are so tolerant, why have there been so many holy wars? The Crusades?

Weren't there, like, eight religious wars in France alone just in the late fifteen hundreds?"

"Right, that's a religious war. War is different." Ami's expression communicated that she understood how nuts her answer sounded. "They have rules about interfering with each other's followers and dismissing each other's beliefs. Waging war on one another's followers?" she held up her hands and shrugged. "That's apparently allowed."

I blinked. "That's insane. Completely irrational and totally insane."

"It may be, but it's also part of their rules."

I smiled thinly. "And you people wonder why I'm an atheist."

"Well, you may think you're an atheist—and, hey, you may even be one. I'm not one to judge. But you're also—currently—the person with a divine familiar. So whether you believe in them or not, believe in these rules or not? You need to at least understand them. Archie can't pass judgment over the religion Pistachio Waterflash has founded. He couldn't tell you what he thought about it or the problems he had with it."

"But he could eat Pistachio Waterflash," I deadpanned. "He couldn't tell me why he was upset, but he could tear a pixie limb from limb."

Ami nodded. "Apparently so."

"This is why I stick with potions," Althea murmured. "They're much easier to understand. They make so much more sense than religious philosophy and dogma."

THANKS TO AUNT GWENNIE, there was hot food for us with a tall glass of fresh lemonade. She watched Althea and me for some time, then said, "When you get done, I have a black forest cake for dessert if you're still hungry."

I shook my head. "Oh, Aunt Gwennie, it's after ten o'clock. If I have black forest cake, I'll be up with heartburn all night."

She came forward and put her hand on my shoulder. "You know, you have a sister that can whip up an antacid that would put the latest and greatest human prescriptions to shame." Aunt Gwennie nodded toward Althea, who was daintily eating barbecued chicken skewers. "You need to start leaning on us, Astra. The same way you leaned on your fellow soldiers at the ministry."

"I do! Well, okay, I don't do it a whole lot—but I'm getting a lot better."

"You are, dear." She sat down at the table and folded her hands. "A pixie war in Central Florida." Aunt Gwennie made a tsk-tsk sound. "I had hoped once the Witches' Council was gone, these types of things would go with them."

"People will always get annoyed at other people, Aunt Gwennie," Althea shrugged. "It's not like that's ever gonna change."

"This is more than an annoyance, child."

"But it's less than a war," Althea told Aunt Gwennie. "At least at this point. Right now, we just have six pixies unhappy with their male leader and a male leader who pixie-dusted four women into followers. Worse things have happened."

"True, but these kinds of conflicts are never good. Large or small, war or skirmish. It threatens the peace in the area. A peace we've worked hard for."

"This isn't so much a war as a civil war, really." I slipped a piece of chicken off the skewer and popped it in my mouth. After swallowing, I asked, "Did you guys have much interaction with the pixies before this? They seemed to know who we were, but not firsthand."

"The pixies were very isolated. Everyone was, of course, when the Witches' Council ruled the paranormals." Althea nodded in agreement as Aunt Gwennie spoke. "Witches could get away with being recognized for what they were by humans, and that's only thanks to the human witches. We simply blended in, and as long as we didn't make any trouble? They—well, you, I suppose—left us alone. It wasn't so for the other paranormal races." My aunt raised her eyebrow. "Surely you would know more about this than us, Astra. After all, you were part of their government."

"Not that part," I told her. "I chased fugitives. The judicial side of the government wrote a warrant for somebody for something. I got assigned to go find that somebody, and I did." I shrugged. "It wasn't really any more complicated than that. I wasn't involved in the trials. I was more of a bounty hunter on salary, really."

"Just out of curiosity, how many of the people you hunted down were witches?" Althea asked thoughtfully.

I thought about it. "Very few, actually. Maybe five percent?"

"And that was typical?"

"Of fugitives? Yeah, pretty typical."

"The last paranormal census said witches were forty-five percent of the paranormal population," Aunt Gwennie pointed out. "I suppose the other ninety-five percent of people you apprehended were made up of the other paranormal species?"

I nodded.

"Sounds to me like you know more about it than you think," Althea told me quietly.

Before I could respond, a rock flew through the window.

"Is everyone all right?" I asked my aunt and sister as we came out from under the table. Their faces fearful, they nodded. "I thought the house was warded?"

"The wards protect us against people coming into the house that have evil intentions," Althea explained as she got up and headed toward the broom closet. "I think we may need to rejigger the wording or something. Someone standing in the street with a flamethrower could burn the place down."

"What was that? Was it an accident?" I scanned around the floor and looked for whatever flew into the window hard enough to shatter it. In the corner, underneath the lip of the cabinet, sat a large gray rock with a rubber band wrapped around it. I could clearly see a piece of paper, folded, tucked inside. "I got it."

Retrieving the rock, I pulled out the paper and unrolled it. "If you don't bring my sister out right now, I will find a way to get in there. Even if I have to hire a rogue witch to break your wards," I read out loud. "Rex."

"Who's Rex?" Aunt Gwennie asked, frowning.

"Emma's brother."

"Her brother?" Aunt Gwennie turned to look at the window. "Why didn't he just come to the door and knock like a normal person? Was this necessary?"

"Because he's not a normal person," I told her. "He's a vampire."

"Oh. He's a vampire," Aunt Gwennie sighed. "That explains it. That young man can't even get on the property, much less to the door."

"We warded the whole property against other paranormals," Althea explained. "Not just the house, but the entire property. They can't come here unless we walk them across the boundary line. Which is, like I said, at the end of the property."

I stared at the two. "And you two were giving

me crap just a minute ago about working for an intolerant administration? Seriously?"

"We didn't give you crap," my aunt told me, offended.

"To be fair, Aunt Gwennie, I was kind of about to." Althea pointed at me. "Valid point to make, sis. Regardless, the dude can't get in. And if he tries, it's gonna hurt."

"I'll go get him—"

"Wait a minute, you can't go get him." My sister's eyes widened. "He's a vampire! Are you crazy? They're bloodthirsty killers."

"He's Emma's brother," I told Althea. "If he found her here, that means he's given her a little bit of his blood so he can keep tabs on her. And if that's the case, he knows there's something wrong with her. And if that's the case?" I pointed. "My bet is he means it when he says he's getting in here one way or another."

"They can do that? Track humans like that?" Aunt Gwennie asked.

"Yes, they can do that, and a whole lot more. But so can we. What's the difference?"

Aunt Gwennie's face half turned away from me. "Maybe we should get your mother—"

I had lived among other paranormals for so long I'd forgotten this fear and prejudice existed

—firmly—outside of Imperatorial City in the witch community. As much as people disliked the Witches' Council, their supremacist ideals (that witches were the rightful rulers of all the paranormal world) produced a people full of arrogance against weaker supernatural species and a deep fear of species with equal strength.

And, apparently, this prejudice was within my own family.

"You guys are the picture of tolerance up until you actually have to deal with one of these other paranormal species that make you a little uncomfortable," I told them both. "He's not 'a vampire.' He's Emma's brother, she's in trouble, and he's worried. That's why he's here. You want me to, what, leave him outside standing at the curb because you have a general concern about vampires?"

"They kill people!" Althea told me.

"I've killed people," I told her. "You want me to go stand by the curb?"

We had talked little about my military service. None of my family asked specifics about what I'd done, and I hadn't volunteered much information. But I'd been a soldier chasing fugitives.

Sure, the Witches' Council was corrupt as all

get out. A lot of the people they sent us after? They didn't deserve it.

But a lot of them? They did.

And a lot of them hid from us among friends of theirs who also deserved it.

I didn't kill many people, and I never killed unnecessarily.

But I'd taken people's lives.

Other paranormals. Other witches. A few people in the wrong place at the wrong time. I never started the fights and never went in looking for one. I was not one of those people that started a mission looking for it to get violent. Wanting that to happen? Never me. But if violence found me?

I would not be the one on the ground at the end.

They stared at me as if they'd never seen me before, and the silence was heavy. It seemed to go on forever. Finally, my sister stepped forward.

"Astra, you didn't," Althea whispered. "You're just trying to make a point. That's not you. You couldn't have done that."

"I did, and I have," I responded quietly. "Never wanted to; it was always something I felt bad about, but sometimes? Sometimes it's just necessary. Wish it wasn't. I wish we lived in a world where it wasn't necessary. But sometimes it is, and when it is, there have to be people prepared to act."

"Oh, Astra," Aunt Gwennie said, reaching for me.

"No, now, look." I held up my hands and tilted my head. "It appears to me I have a lot more experience with other paranormals than any of you. Book learning only gets you so far. Vampires are like anyone else—they're just people. Some are good, some are bad. I don't know which Rex is, but I do know he's Emma's brother, and he's worried about her. We owe it to her to give him the benefit of the doubt."

Aunt Gwennie and Althea glanced at one another, their expressions unsure.

"If he makes a move, I can take him down. None of you will be in any danger. I can assure you of that." They turned and stared at me. "Are we agreed?"

They nodded, but they didn't look sure of their answer.

"Stay here. I'll be back."

As I left the house, I was sure one of them was running to get my mother.

"REX?" I stopped at the edge of the grass, just before the boundary.

I was confident, but I wasn't stupid.

"You're Astra Arden," the vampire responded, his voice Frank Sinatra smooth.

"I am."

Rex was tall, lean, with dark brown eyes that seemed to burn straight into my soul. His skin was clear and smooth, freshly shaved, his brown hair tousled by the wind he had no doubt sailed through faster than the human eye could see to get here from Las Vegas. He was, like all vampires, overpoweringly handsome.

You could take the most awkward, unattractive human, turn them into a vampire, and they inevitably became the most charming, elegant, attractive being. I always figured it had something to do with the vampire's need to attract humans to feed. "I sensed that my sister was in trouble and came to find her. She wasn't at her apartment." He glanced toward Arden House. "She's in there, isn't she?"

"She is," I told him.

"Have you hurt her?" he asked, leaning in slightly. Rex's voice was only mildly threatening.

"Emma is my friend. I would never hurt her."

He considered me with those intense brown

eyes for a few seconds and then tilted his head. "She claimed that to me, and yet I'm here. I sense her in danger." Rex's face darkened as he stared intently at me. "How do you explain this?"

"That, my friend, would take a while."

A pause and stillness again. "Are we friends, Astra Arden?"

Well, Rex, that depends on you. Are you planning on drinking my entire family? Then no, we're probably not friends.

I took a deep breath and made my overture to the vampire.

"I'd like us to be. You're the brother of my closest human friend and partner. I'd like to be able to invite you in—past our wards—and know that my three sisters, my aunt, and my mother would be safe. Oh, and my owl." I stared into the stranger's face trying to read his intentions, but he was a vampire. Their intentions were inscrutable. "Can I do that? Can you give me assurances that you'll harm no one on this property? And if you do, can I trust those assurances?"

Thin frown lines appeared. "I cannot promise anything if I find you harmed my sister."

"You won't. I haven't. And no one in that house has or would."

202 | LEANNE LEEDS

His face was ordinary and yet powerfully attractive. It was a bizarre paradox. Vampires were strange, strange creatures. Everything about them at first glance seemed balanced, even unassuming. But if you watched them for a while, their stillness and quiet would nag at you. Something would seem off, wrong, odd—even if you couldn't reasonably determine what it was. Your subconscious could sense the genteel mask hiding great chaos just beneath the surface—even as it struggled how to warn you of the maelstrom.

It was a chaos and frenzy only their victims ever saw, and they didn't live long enough to tell anybody what it looked like.

"I am going to trust what you say, for now, Astra Arden. I assure you that if you invite me in, I will not harm anyone who shares the space with me within the wards. At least, while they are within the wards," Rex told me with a gentle strength. "Is this oath enough for you?"

I stared into the vampire's eyes and felt a flutter deep in my chest. Their powers of attraction were not quite as strong on witches as they were on humans, not magical. However, vampires were still the walking definition of "sexy beast." It was hard to ignore Rex's magnetism. "It's enough." I reached out my gloved hand. "Emma's sleeping, but I'll bring you to her."

"Do you know what's happened to my sister?"

"I think so," I told him as he stepped across. "But I'm not sure what to do about it."

CHAPTER THIRTEEN

"You might've found me to ask whether I would be all right with having a vampire in my home, Astra," my mother said with imperious politeness.

"Didn't have time." I pointed to the broken window.

My sisters must have warned her Rex would be coming in the house because she was waiting, leaning against the archway frame, with her softly judgmental game face on. The archway leads to the hallway that leads to Emma and Alice sleeping on the sofa. It was a place I didn't think it was wise to stand, but my mother had her own way of doing things.

I suppose I should be grateful she wasn't

standing with arms outstretched shouting "You shall not pass!" like Gandalf to the Balrog in *Lord of the Rings*.

Not that Rex was a Balrog.

Archie perched beside her, his face unreadable.

"I'm sorry, Mother. I wasn't aware at the start of this evening we banned paranormals from the house," I responded, trying desperately not to sound patronizing. I then turned to Archie. "Speaking of that, it makes me wonder how you got in here without being walked in. If non-witch paranormals can't cross the boundary line."

Archie had shown up on the front porch alone.

Or so it seemed at the time, anyway.

"I am the goddess's own owl," Archie answered with a shrug. "This is the goddess's own temple with the goddess's own high priestess." He held out a wing and tilted his head. "Obviously, I didn't have a problem. I wouldn't be very much use if wards actually worked on me, now, would I?"

Well, that was presumptuous. He wasn't a whole lot of use today.

The two stood tall like they owned the place. Which, okay, in my mother's case—she did.

Archie's expression was difficult to read. I couldn't tell precisely what he was thinking, but he didn't seem alarmed by Rex's presence in the least.

My mother, on the other hand, kept her wide eyes glued to the vampire with a cold, uneasy expression.

Rex waited, expectantly, for my mother to move out of his way. I was sure his highly evolved senses had zeroed in on Emma already. Because of that, he knew (without my mother having to say a word) she was blocking him from entering the living room. When she didn't move, Rex's eyes traveled over her and Archie. "Do I have reason to be concerned here, priestess?"

"If you're asking whether I am going to stake you where you stand, no, vampire. You have nothing to worry about. For the moment." The tone of her voice didn't make it sound like he had nothing to worry about.

"Mom, he's just here to check on his sister. Let's let him do that."

My mother turned toward me sharply. "You've done enough for one evening, Astra," she warned me. "Stay out of this."

I knew her well enough to know she was furious at me for letting Rex in the door, and it seemed a ridiculous overreaction. For a split second, my anger flared.

This was ridiculous—and speciesist. There were hundreds of paranormals across the world far more dangerous than a vampire. And vampires were previously human—and very similar to witches in vestiges of humanity. Just because they drink blood...I mean, I didn't blame Rex for his diet any more than I blamed Archie. This man—vampire, whatever—was first and foremost Emma's brother.

This whole thing? My mother's reaction? It was ridiculous.

And, by the way, it also showed a complete lack of confidence in my ability to kick his butt. Which was disappointing, since I was sure I could take him.

Rex stared at my mother with an unnerving intensity. "I gave your daughter certain assurances. I oathed to Astra that I would harm no one on this property while I was here. I intend to keep my word, priestess."

I nodded to confirm.

"I assume you extracted similar oaths from her?" my mother asked. "It would make no sense for you to walk into a temple without them."

"No."

Her eyebrow raised. "No? You just walked into a house with multiple witches and didn't bother to ensure your own safety by oath?" Althea and Ami silently watched the exchange between our mother and the vampire. "Why would you do that?"

A brief half-smile flashed across his handsome face. "With respect, I don't need to extract oaths to ensure my own safety," Rex said, his gaze passing over everyone gathered. My mother tensed at his low-key brag, but he raised his hand. "But I am aware of who you are and that you owe me guest-friendship. Your own goddess demonstrated what this entailed when she visited Ithaca. If I asked for more than that, it would be disrespectful to your own professed beliefs."

"And you care about respecting our beliefs?"

"I have no desire to cause offense."

I looked back and forth between them, trying to figure out what they were talking about. What was guest-friendship? And why hadn't anyone issued me a house handbook when I came home so I wouldn't be caught unaware of the multitude of rules? I swear, my mother had more rules than the military.

Althea caught my look of confusion and edged

toward me. "The Odyssey," she whispered. "Didn't you ever read it?"

"Why on earth would I read that dusty old tome? Isn't it, like, a bazillion words?" My sister's brow wrinkled. "Yes, yes, I know you all have to read it. I know I was supposed to. I didn't. What is Rex talking about?"

"Athena visited Ithaca disguised as Mentes, a hero," Althea explained. Though she was still whispering, my sister had the attention of everyone in the room. "In the story, they make it clear that only one guy treated her with proper respect as a guest. From there, we got the rules of guest-friendship. Once Rex crossed the threshold, we became obligated to feed him, give him a drink, and offer him a place to sleep equal to or better than our own sleeping quarters. Treat him like royalty. Basically."

"And this is a religious obligation?" I asked. "Is he right about that?"

"Alcinous considered hospitality part of his sacred duty to the gods, and so hospitality became our sacred duty, as well," she finished. "It has been so ever since."

"So the vampire is right." I pushed again.

"Yes."

"Any other questions, Astra?" my mother asked tartly.

"Actually, I think I do," I said, suddenly realizing the full impact of the obligation and obstacles my mother had deliberately erected to make sure she wouldn't have to. "So, you guys have some religious obligation of hospitality to anyone that shows up here, but you created wards to keep out all paranormals so none of them could ever show up here?" I paused, but no one answered me. "Do I have that right?"

Rex shot me a brief look of amusement.

My sister met my eyes. "Well, it's not, like, exactly that way," Ami said slowly. Then she frowned. "At least I don't think it is. The way you said it sounds bad." Ami looked at my mother. "Mom?"

My mother's face was impassive, but Althea's expression told me she'd figured out long before that they complied with the "rules" of hospitality without the burden of being hospitable. I shook my head. "Wow. That's some serious technicality twisting there, Mom. Practically military-like in its—"

A sound of impatience, soft as a summer's breeze, slipped from the lips of the vampire. "While all this discussion of priestess-witch customs is truly fascinating, now that we've established your obligations and mine?" Rex flexed his hands. "I'd like to see my sister."

The frustration twisted my mother's face, but she took a deep breath.

Then she nodded.

Then she stepped aside.

"HOW DID HE WIND UP HERE?" Archie asked.

"He's a vampire?" Turning, I watched Emma and Rex. She was still asleep on the couch snoring peacefully. He crouched down in front of her, his hands resting lightly on her knees. "He probably gave Emma some of his blood so he could keep tabs on her. He knew there was something off, and he used his supersonic travel power to get here quick." Turning back, I raised my eyebrow. "I don't want to talk about him right now. I want to talk about you."

"Oh?" Archie asked distractedly.

"How am I supposed to trust you if you can't tell me what's going on?" I asked him. "I never would've brought you...Actually, I didn't bring you into the pixie area, now that I think about it. You just decided to invade their home turf all on your own." I crossed my arms. "I was just starting to trust you, Archie, and then you pull a stunt like this."

He shrugged. "If I'd eaten him, your case would have been solved."

"You're telling me Pistachio Waterflash is going to try and kill Alice?"

"Well, it makes sense, doesn't it?" the owl asked with arrogant confidence. "Ami told me that she told you what I told your mother. Doesn't that solve the case?" He swung his head with an exaggerated flare of feathers. "Some guy that would drug women would obviously kill them. I mean, it's the first step on a—"

"That's a little black-and-white. And assumptive."

"Of course it's not," he responded with another shake of feathers. "It's obvious to me."

"Is it now? Do you know anything else that Ami didn't tell me?" I asked him.

His big owl eyes blinked. "What do you mean?"

"What I mean is you've given me absolutely no evidence that Pistachio Waterflash wants Alice dead. All you've brought to the table is that he's a narcissistic jerk trying to start a cult of women that worship him. Good information to have, but

I wound up getting it anyway—from the rebel pixies." I raised my eyebrow. "I also hate to tell you this, Archie, but what he's doing doesn't exactly make him super unique. I mean, the sun dust he's using and the fact that he's a pixie make him unique. But his motivations?" I held my hands up. "Not really. He's just a narcissistic man with entitlement issues. It doesn't mean he's a murderer."

Another exaggerated blink. "You don't like men very much, do you?"

Where on earth did that come from? "I like decent men just fine. He's not a decent man. But Althea and I just spent an evening with six female pixies out to stop their chieftain from starting the Casanova Cult with their magic. There's more going on here than 'Pistachio Waterflash is a big dumb jerk,'" I told the owl. "Althea and I spotted a pixie stealing fuel injectors from all the construction equipment at a site Alice ultimately owns."

"What does that have to do with anything?"

I pointed and nodded. "See, that's the type of question you should be asking. I don't know yet, but I'm pretty sure eating Pistachio Waterflash wouldn't get us any closer to knowing the answer." For a small fraction of a second, the fiery arrogance in the owl's eye was clouded by uncertainty. "You see what I mean now?"

"Maybe," he murmured.

"And I have more news for you. The pixies said there are four women under sun dust control. Well, I should clarify—that's what the rebel pixies think, anyway. Alice was the first. Emma, obviously." I gestured toward the couch. "One woman they were not aware of and hadn't been able to identify."

"The rebel pixies? Sounds like a grunge band." The owl frowned. "You said four. That's three."

"The fourth is Meryl Hawkins. She's a reporter for the *Forkbridge Gazette*. The one that interviewed Emma and me this morning."

Archie turned suddenly back toward me. An exaggerated blink. "Well, that doesn't seem random. That doesn't seem random at all. Those three people all being drugged and under one person's control?"

Now it was my turn to blink. He was right. "An heiress, a reporter, a detective?" I crossed my arms. "No, now that you mention it…that doesn't seem random at all, does it?"

"So which pixies sabotaged the construction equipment? The rebel pixies, or the sun-dust narcissist pixie?"

I looked back at Archie with embarrassment.

Archie raised what passed for an eyebrow on an owl. "Didn't you go into pixie territory specifically to investigate what pixie sabotaged the equipment?"

"We did, but somehow, we never quite... covered that. With them."

"So you don't even know which side wanted the construction equipment disabled?" Archie looked vaguely surprised. "Maybe you should make sure you have all your ducks in a row before you start giving divine creatures guff for trying to solve the case in a way that wasn't perfectly to your liking." I watched the raptor as he pulled his arrogance back together without effort. "So what now, genius?"

"Besides you working on your people skills?"

"Haha."

"I'm going to talk to Althea about an antidote for the sun dust. I don't know what her capabilities are, but she seems to be pretty adept at this potion stuff. Maybe she can come up with a way to break whatever spell Emma and Alice are under."

Archie nodded. "You think that will save Alice?"

"I think we have a better shot of saving Alice if

she's not drooling and giggling over Pistachio Waterflash. But no, I have a feeling the threat to Alice is more tangible than that." I looked back at the sleeping heiress. I didn't know why the two were sleeping or what control—if any—Pistachio had her under. And I didn't like how much I didn't know.

"There's just too much swirling around her—a pixie war, the CEO of her company under investigation, being targeted by Pistachio. Add in the sabotage at the construction site, the sun-dusted reporter...it feels like something's going on here that we're all missing."

"There's always something going on we're all missing."

REX STEPPED AWAY from Emma and made his way to where Archie and I were talking. "She is deeply asleep and dreaming of some man. A pixie, I believe."

"Green hair?" I asked Rex. He nodded. "Pistachio Waterflash."

"The other one on the couch is dreaming of him as well." Rex gestured to a chair next to Archie and me, and I nodded. He moved so quietly the chair didn't even creak when he sat down. "They are not in any specific danger that I can sense, but they are not under their own control completely. There is something or someone else within their minds." His downcast eyes moved from me to Archie. "I would like to help you uncover the truth of the situation you've been discussing."

"What situation?" Archie asked with casual dismissal. "We haven't been discussing a situation."

I smiled at the bird. "Vampires have exceptional hearing. It's quite likely Rex could tell us what the people three houses away are discussing over the dinner table without exerting much effort." I glanced at the clock and sighed. "Or maybe while they're brushing their teeth getting ready for bed? Wow, it's late."

"For you, perhaps," Rex said with one of his brief smiles. He turned toward Archie. "Astra is right. I heard every word that the two of you said. I also heard every word they said," Rex shared as he glanced at my mother and two sisters across the room. They were about as far from the vampire as they could be and still be in the room. "I'm sure that Astra is quite capable, but I know that there is a clock ticking on that woman's life, and you may be at a disadvantage because of my sister's condition. You have little police backup without Emma."

"How are you going to give me police backup?" I asked him.

"I won't. But I'm not bound by legal rules." He paused. "That might be useful."

"Pardon me for saying so, but you're talking like you know everything going on here." Rex looked up at me quickly and then dropped his eyes again. His mouth twitched. "Nothing to say?"

"I have certain abilities. Some because I'm a vampire, and some because I am the type of vampire I am. I am aware of what you are, what the owl is. Once I sensed my sister was in trouble, I focused heavily on hearing what was going on around her." When he spoke, his voice had a toneless quality. He seemed tired.

"Are you telling me that you can use Emma like a spy bug?" I asked him, shocked. Even Archie looked surprised. "You can hear what she hears? See what she sees?"

He nodded. "It's quite similar to your power. Emma is the only 'object' I can see and hear through, and I don't need to be touching her to do so." He stopped talking and looked up at me to see how I was taking what he said. "Once there were more, but since I left the organization that turned me, it's only Emma. And it's only to ensure her safety."

In the silence that followed, I asked with a slightly accusing tone: "Does she know this?"

"She knows that we are bonded. Emma is aware of many of my powers." His mouth snapped open, and his fangs glinted at me in the dim light of the living room. Just as quickly, it closed, and his face melted into impassivity. "She knows what I am."

"Look, as much as I would like to help, I don't know you—"

"And as much as I would like to tell you I would stay out of your way? I won't. My offer was politeness, but that is my sister, and she is in trouble," he told me, his voice strong and determined. "It would probably be more useful if we work together, but mark my words, Astra Arden, Archimedes—I am going to find who did this to my sister. With or without your assistance."

I paused and thought of all the reasons working with the vampire was a horrible idea. They couldn't always be trusted. At times, they would tell the truth in a way that left you with more questions than answers. They could, obviously, be dangerous.

And this wasn't just a vampire. This was an ex-mafia vampire.

But it was for all those reasons he could be helpful. Hell, just his super hearing might quickly uncover what was going on with Meryl Hawkins.

"Deal," I told him. He nodded.

I glanced across the room and saw my mother's eyes blazing with panic.

"By the way," Archie asked the vampire casually. "How are you able to hear me talk?"

I felt the shock zip through my body like a lightning bolt.

I combed my memory for the past several minutes of interaction. I realized the vampire and the owl had been conversing. I saw, heard, observed, and participated in that conversation without ever realizing none of it should be happening.

"No idea," Rex responded. "Can't everyone?"

"No. Just the women of this family," I responded.

"Curious," the vampire said and shrugged.

"Huh," Archie added, also shrugging.

The two were masters of understatement.

CHAPTER FOURTEEN

I pretended to be oblivious to the sour look on my mother's face. She pretended to be oblivious to the fact that I would do exactly what I wanted, with or without her input.

Rex was right. We were on a clock, and that clock was ticking down. I took my job seriously—the whole "save someone when a card with a star glowed" thing—but my nerves ratcheted up to a slightly higher level now that Emma was affected by whatever this was.

I glanced over at her. Why the heck was she sleeping?

"She's peaceful, for now," Rex assured me.

I glanced at Emma's brother. He was another reason I was raring to go.

I'd never gotten to use a vampire in an investigation. There were very few employed by the military—vampires aren't exactly joiners. The ones that signed up were always being deployed on some weird black ops mission the rest of us never heard about. I'd heard rumors that a vampire assistant on a case was a quick solve guarantee. So quick you might even get time off afterward.

"Do you have some plan, Astra?" my mother asked me (in a way that made me think she already knew I did, and she was hoping I would think better of it).

Mom's expression was easy to read.

She wanted the vampire out of her house and away from her daughters.

Unfortunately for my mother, Rex represented a tantalizing possibility for surveillance, and there was precisely zero chance I'd pass up the opportunity his involvement presented.

I took a deep breath. "I think Althea needs to focus on finding some sort of cure for whatever this is," I said, waving at Alice and Emma. Althea nodded in response. "Rex and I can make it to the

Punktex offices on the outskirts of town within twenty minutes, and then we'll head back into the swamp. If we stop yammering, he and I should be able to accomplish quite a bit before dawn—"

"The grocery chain?" the vampire asked, his expression slightly confused. "You want to go to a grocery store chain's office in the middle of the night?"

"She owns it," I told him, pointing toward Alice. "This whole thing started with her. Maybe if we break in and ransack the place, we can find some evidence—"

"You can't break the law," my mother informed me.

"Look, I don't really plan to ransack the place. Just slip in and have a look around, see what we can find." I pointed to Archie. "As to your point, I'm breaking the law just by having an owl."

"You make me sound like such a rebel," Archie noted. He looked pleased.

My mother kept her eyes on me. "You know what I mean."

"I do." You mean I should play it safe and do what you say. "But I can, and I'm going to," I informed her in a stern voice. "There's a reason the Vegas mafia created an army of vampires to do their bidding." Rex looked surprised I knew of his history. "I spent fifteen years sneaking into places no one knew I'd ever visited. Between the two of us?" I glanced at Rex. "No one will even know we were there."

"But you work for the police department," Aunt Gwennie said. "What if you get caught and lose your job?"

"I don't work as a police officer. And as a consultant? It's not my responsibility to uphold the law. Just assist the people that do." The expressions staring back at me ranged from disapproving to worried. "Guys. I promise. I was in the military, I know how to read a contract. I don't even have a moral turpitude clause in the thing."

"What's moral turpitude?" Althea asked.

"A vague sounding thing that means you did something bad, and it violates the morals of the community, I think," Aunt Gwennie told her.

"Wouldn't her outfit qualify?" Archie asked wryly.

"As far as my job is concerned, I'm just some random citizen of Forkbridge." Aunt Gwennie nodded slowly, but my mother and I faced each other in silence. "Which job is more important, Mom? The job with Emma or the job your goddess assigned me?"

That caught her off guard.

Rex watched my family debate the ethical and moral boundaries of my investigative techniques, his face unreadable.

Which, again, he's a vampire. His face being unreadable is kind of just his face.

My mother looked at Rex with suspicion. "I don't like the idea of you going off with a vampire by yourself. No offense meant."

"I'm not sensitive," the vampire responded evenly to my mother's suspicion.

"Is that all?" I asked, throwing up my hands and feigning relief. "That's easy. We can solve that in a second."

"How do you propose we do that?" my mother asked.

"Which one of my younger sisters would you like me to take on this illegal adventure?" I waved my arm at Althea and Ami. "Do you want me to drag Ami along on her first break-in? I mean, she's not even legal to go into a bar yet, but sure." I smiled. "Let's take her on her first burglary. I'm sure she can learn as she goes. Althea's busy, so how about Ayla? Want me to go get the thirteen-year-old out of bed? She snuck into my Jeep last time. Might be easier just to take her." I paused. "You tell me, Mom. Which one should I take?"

My mother's face looked like it'd been on the receiving end of a palm strike to the nose. Mom wasn't used to being spoken to like this, and everything in her posture recoiled from me. "I don't like your tone, young lady."

Of course she didn't.

"Then start being serious, Mom. Or start taking me seriously. I was in the military; he's ex-mafia. This won't be the first rodeo for either one of us." My mother's eyes narrowed. "The clock is ticking, and we have to figure out where this threat is coming from. Definitively. I don't have time to do 'Ami's first burglary.' She's not trained; she has no experience at this—"

"I really don't want to break into an office building," Ami murmured.

"—and by the way, your paranoia that I can't defend myself against a vampire? Offensive. Really offensive," I told her curtly.

"No one is trying to offend you, Astra, dear," Mom responded coldly.

"And I'm not trying to offend you." I really wasn't. But I wasn't exactly trying to be delicate with her feelings, either. "But I know what I'm doing. This is my lane. I know how to drive in it."

Rex and I jumped into the Jeep. I reached forward to start the engine and then paused. Holding up my finger, I climbed into the back and looked under anything and everything not nailed down. I even opened the toolbox.

"Sorry," I told him, sliding back into the front seat. He raised his eyebrow. "My thirteen-year-old sister. She has a habit of sneaking into the Jeep just when things are getting risky or dangerous."

"Ah. Understood. Where is this office?"

"About fifteen minutes away. At least, the way I drive."

"Nice Jeep," he said.

"Thanks."

We both fell silent for a bit. I thought about how much more difficult this was turning out to be, especially with Emma out of commission.

I wasn't a detective. The nuances of clues and things pointing to a guilty party, deciding who needed to be caught? That wasn't anything I'd had to deal with before, not really. My job at the ministry involved going after a target. I got a file with a name, information, a picture. It wasn't easy, but…well, I never had to decide who that target would be.

"Are you all right?" Rex asked me, his voice deeply concerned.

I glanced at Rex. Vampires were masters of mimicry—they could present as concerned, caring, loving even if there wasn't a bone in their body legitimately feeling that way. Evolutionary sociopaths, my trainer called them. My mother was right, honestly, to be a little worried. His deep concern for me was likely nothing more than his way of building rapport because he needed me.

Because if he didn't need me?

He wouldn't be here.

"Right now, I really wish your sister would wake up and help me out here," I said, my fingers tightening around the steering wheel. "I was just thinking about the fact that my skill set lies in chasing down someone already known. I don't have a whole lot of experience in playing Colombo. I feel like I'm just floundering, here, trying to figure out what's going on."

"You have some skills that apply to the current situation," Rex pointed out. "You always knew who you were assigned to bring in, but you still had to use your wits to track them down. Surely, you questioned people they knew or their co-

conspirators. Had to decide who was lying, who was telling the truth."

I'd forgotten Rex was the one that told Emma who I was and what I used to do. She mentioned that he had been one of the vampires turned by a crime family in Las Vegas, and it made sense they would know exactly who we were. "Okay, yes, if they had co-conspirators, I did—"

"That's right, I forgot," he said with a quick shake of his head. "You worked for the Witches' Council. Very few that you chased had committed crimes, much less had co-conspirators." The tone in his voice made it clear he wasn't a fan.

"And you worked for the mob," I pointed out.

"I did, indeed," he admitted.

"So, I signed up to protect paranormals. I joined the military with the best of intentions. The leadership being completely corrupt wasn't my fault." I glanced at him. "What's your excuse?"

He didn't respond.

Despite my bite-back, Rex and I were likely far more similar than I ever would've suspected back when I was working for the military. We both carried out the whims of narcissistic leaders who felt entitled to control other people. We both punished those that didn't do precisely what those leaders thought they should.

"How, exactly, did my sister wind up in a coma on your couch?" Rex asked after a certain amount of silence.

"I don't really know. When we met with the rebel pixies in the swamp, they said that their leader— a chieftain named Pistachio Waterflash — was using sacred water and pixie dust combined to bring women under his control." I exited off the highway toward Forkbridge's relatively small business park. "I've never heard of anything like it, and I'm not sure the pixies had either, to be honest."

"Don't you have the power of psychometry?" Rex asked.

"I do," I told him.

"Why didn't you just read my sister to find out when it happened?"

"Since you're looking through her eyes and ears all the time, why don't you just tell me when it happened?" I glanced at the passenger seat.

He glared at me. "If I knew what was going on, don't you think I would've done something about it already? It doesn't work like that. I don't know everything she's done and everything she's seen and everything she's talked about with everyone she meets. I can connect with her, check on her, but I don't spend all day spying on my sister." He shifted in the seat. "Besides, I didn't know there was anything to be concerned about until it had already happened."

"Here's what I know." We pulled into the parking lot next to a dark office building. Aside from a few older-model cars, it was empty. "The glowing star card came up in Alice Windrow's reading. That means that within seventy-two hours, she's going to be dead, and the goddess Athena doesn't want that to happen. Right now, she's the sole private owner of Punktex. She became the sole private owner after her parents inherited the ownership from a distant relative. They were killed soon after. I mean, like, within a few weeks of inheriting the company."

"What does that have to do with pixies?" Rex asked, looking confused.

"I don't entirely know. There could be two things going on here since pixies aren't exactly known for playing a long game. With the new rules around interacting with humans, though?" I held up my hands. "I just don't know. But Alice is a pixie follower."

"What's a pixie follower?"

"Someone who follows the path of the pixies."

His brows drew together. "The path of the pixies? Is that a thing?"

"A new religion, apparently. Yeah, I don't know. Not important. Anyway, Alice seemed pretty normal when she got her reading, but later she started acting...I don't know, giddy? Obsessed? And when she and Emma got together, it was like whatever crazy obsession the two of them had for Pistachio Waterflash? It was doubled. And if the star card thing glowed and she started acting like a nutter thanks to the pixies, I feel like it has to be related."

"If the rebel pixies you met with are correct, that means the two of them are doused with whatever this pixie potion is," he said. I nodded. "And we don't have any idea why Emma was doused with this. Could it have just rubbed off on her accidentally?"

"Not if the rebel pixies are telling the truth. Pistachio touched her arm in this, like, creepy way when we met with him," I explained. "My guess is that's when it happened."

"Okay," he nodded. "But why?"

"So, that's where we're getting into theory." I leaned back and tapped the steering wheel. "I don't know anything for sure. We said very little to the chieftain beyond asking him about Alice

Windrow." I raised my eyebrow. "What better way to slow down an investigation into what you're doing than to drug the female detective investigating the case?"

Rex thought about it for a moment. "Why not drug you?" he asked.

I sniffed. Maybe it was because I detected the distinct odor of suspicion coming off the vampire. Or, you know, allergies.

"I don't know. Maybe witches are immune. Maybe he didn't see me as a threat. For whatever reason, I am not dazzled by Pistachio Waterflash. But your sister is."

"So what conspiracy do you think he's trying to cover up?"

"This is a guess," I said and pointed to the building. "Paul Wakefield, the CEO of Punktex, would basically get all control of the company if something permanent were to happen to Alice Windrow. He's the only one with clear motivation to want her dead. I don't know how he's linked to the pixies, but starting there seems like a good idea."

"And you think we will find evidence of something in there?"

"I think it's better than poking around a swamp and trusting pixies."

We didn't sneak into the building.

We walked in through the front door.

Vampires had a few extremely useful powers, one of which was a form of hypnosis. Originally used to lure in and ensnare their victims, now they tended to use the ability to walk right into blood banks seemingly undetected.

Well, some of them.

I'm sure some still used their powers to gain victims. There are always stubborn stragglers on any evolutionary path bringing up the rear.

I wasn't sure which one Rex was, and I didn't want to ask.

In any case, Rex Sullivan dazzled the security guard with his vampire charms, causing the young man to slip into a deep sleep right at his desk.

"I'll take care of the security cameras," Rex told me, stepping around the desk and gently moving the snoring security guard. Suddenly, he frowned. "Astra? These cameras have been turned off already." He looked up at me. "The whole bank of them. They're all black."

"Did sleeping beauty over there knock into a switch when he fell asleep?" I asked.

The vampire scanned the desk and found the button that turned the security cameras off and on. "No, he couldn't have. I was watching him."

I came around the back of the desk. "Well, turn them on. Let's see if anything is going on. If someone turned them off deliberately, somebody is trying to hide something."

Rex nodded and flipped the switch. The grainy images flickered gray-blue snow, then lines, and then came into focus. Ten cameras focused on ten places in this relatively small building. All seemingly empty—

"There," he said quietly, pointing. "There are people in that office."

"Two people," I said, leaning forward.

Then I blushed.

The camera was not high definition, and I couldn't identify the two people locked in a heated embrace on a couch in a large office. I could tell enough to surmise the visual content of the confab would have gotten the security feed an R rating from the Motion Picture Association of America. At the very least.

"Why would someone meet late at night in an office?" Rex asked.

I stared at the vampire. You lived in Vegas, the city of sin. Really? You can't think of any reason two people would be *in flagrante delicto* on an uncomfortable office couch in the middle of the night? Really?

That's what I wanted to say, but I needed the vampire.

So I didn't say it.

"Maybe they were working late, and one thing led to another. Maybe this is an ongoing affair, and they meet here to avoid detection." I shrugged. "No idea, but we need to go and find out. Judging by the furniture, that's an executive office." No one other than executives had couches in their office. At least not in my experience. "That could be Paul Wakefield. And if it is, I'm going to bet dollars to donuts that woman's not his wife. It could be a pixie."

We crept quietly up the stairway so the elevator would not ding and give away our presence in the building or on the third floor. I'm a little embarrassed to admit that Rex stepped even more softly than I did. I prided myself on my cunning ability to skulk quietly, but the vampire? He elevated it to an art form.

As soon as we opened the stairwell door, we could hear murmured, breathy words from the office down the hall. The hallway was dark. Light from a lamp in the office gave a smoky, dim glow. I pointed toward a corner, and Rex nodded. We tiptoed toward it, but still couldn't see inside.

"Oh, Paul, Paul, Paul," a woman crooned. "You know what we have to do, baby. You know why we have to do it." Heavy panting. "It'll be incredible. Just you and me. Please, baby, you have to do it for me."

The voice, even in its excited state, seemed vaguely familiar. I wracked my brain, but I couldn't quite place it—even though I was sure I'd heard it before.

"I can't. My wife would kill me," Paul responded to his female companion. "I'm already in so much trouble! I could go to jail!"

"No, no, you're not going to go to jail," the woman told him breathlessly. "Those people in Orlando don't know anything about us. I'm sure the accountants just messed up. Everybody loves you, Pauly. One look at that face? How could anyone convict you?" More kissing noises.

I made a face. "Paul Wakefield," I mouthed to Rex.

"But who's the woman?" he mouthed back.

I shrugged. "Clearly not his wife."

"She is not as excited as he is," he said, his eyes sparkling with concentration. "His heart rate is quite elevated. Hers is not. It's like she's playing a role."

Sounded like Paul Wakefield was getting played by a femme fatale.

But who?

And why?

"Oh, Meryl, this is wrong," Paul Wakefield moaned when he came up for breath. "I can't do this to my wife. I just can't!" More smacking sounds demonstrating that despite his protestations, apparently, he could.

"Meryl?" Rex asked.

"Meryl Hawkins," I told him, my eyes narrowing. "Well, that..." I thought for a minute. "Yeah, that doesn't clear anything up at all, really."

CHAPTER FIFTEEN

"I wonder if that woman is even capable of having a relationship with someone that doesn't already have a commitment to someone else," I muttered as Rex concentrated. "Prominent people and adulterous affairs seem to be her hobby."

The two of us sat in the Jeep facing the office building. Yes, there probably were papers in there that would help us. And yes, we did come here to ransack the place. But those papers were likely in the same room with the conflicted couple, and it wasn't worth it to put three people to sleep.

One person having a paranormal experience will think they imagined it.

Three people can compare notes.

Besides, remember when I said vampires could be helpful?

Vampires are telepathic. Like, hugely telepathic. They can read minds. Everyone knows they can read minds. But far lesser-known in the general para-population? They can create illusions in someone's mind to trick them.

Yeah, I know. Crazy, right?

Honestly, I've always suspected the fear of vampires was due more to their telepathic skills than the whole blood drinking thing. Sure, no one wants to be a carbon-based cocktail, but being controlled by something else? If I had to choose one or the other, I'd prefer to be a cocktail.

People know they've been controlled, and they know who directed them, though. So vampires tended to leave that power in their back pocket.

I'm digressing here. Where were we?

Right. Sitting outside the office building. So, the one drawback to the vampire mental eavesdropping? They need physical proximity to the person's mind they're reading. Being close to the target was necessary to get good information, but right outside a building?

That was close enough.

"Her mind isn't filled with all sorts of plans," Rex explained, concentrating. "So, I can't tell you what role she has to play in this, or even whether she has an active role. At least, not yet. I can tell you that she's been deceiving you. The interview that she did this morning?" He glanced over. "That interview was her idea. She used it to get near you and Emma. Her primary goal was to be introduced to you both, not the article itself."

"That had to be when Emma got dusted," I guessed. "But why? Meryl Hawkins isn't connected to any of these people. She's, like, twenty years younger than Paul Wakefield. How did they even meet, much less start an affair?"

"I can't tell you that yet," Rex said. He frowned. "She's not in love with that man. From what I can sense, she doesn't even particularly like him."

"That doesn't necessarily mean she's part of the conspiracy, you know. If there even is a conspiracy. Which we still don't know. Anyway, I don't need a psychic to tell me that she's power and money hungry." I pointed. "He's got both. Maybe this is nothing more than a social climber targeting a man that she thinks is ripe for the picking because he's having marital issues."

Rex looked at me. "You're rather cynical about human motivation."

"I am not," I retorted. "I'm rather cynical about everyone's motivation. Humans, vampires, witches, pixies. My cynicism does not discriminate."

He gazed at me with a contemplative eye. I could sense the telepathic bloodsucker wanted to say something else. Still, before he could decide whether to speak, another impression grabbed his attention. "He's not...wise to her," Rex continued. "In fact, the man thinks the woman truly loves him, and he is torn by the memory of love for his wife and the current love he feels for her."

"I wouldn't think the head of a company would be that naive." Maybe some adulterous secret affairs between younger women and rich older men worked out in the end. In my experience, though, they didn't.

Um, not my personal experience.

I wouldn't touch another woman's husband with a ten-foot pole.

Not all of my fellow soldiers felt the same way.

Rex lifted his chin, his eyes fixed on the third-floor window. "He is naive, though," the vampire disagreed. "This man is not savvy. Just listening to his thoughts the past few minutes, I've gotten a sense of him as a person." He turned. "You say this man has been arrested for embezzling from this company?"

I nodded. "He hasn't been indicted yet, but Emma thinks it's only a matter of time. She talked to some investigators in Orlando earlier today." I looked at my watch. "Well, yesterday now."

"Paul Wakefield believes himself to be an honorable man."

"Lots of dishonorable people believe themselves to be honorable. That doesn't mean anything."

"It's more than that. It's something he works at, prides himself on. I get no sense of greed, no cunning. No avarice that would prompt him to risk prison for the accumulation of money." Rex tilted his head. "He is quite satisfied with his life from a material standpoint. The only point of pain is a disintegrated romantic relationship with his wife. And his commitment toward his marriage hasn't wavered."

"I'd call having your hand down someone's blouse that's not your wife a wavering commitment, Rex." I pointed. "You're telling me the guy upstairs in his office having an affair and cheating on his wife believes himself to be honorable." I rolled my eyes. "Are you sure your telepathic radar isn't on the fritz? Or maybe he's the delusional one."

"Don't believe so. I sense no mental illness."

Exhaling, I glared at him. "You're a psychiatrist now?"

"The woman personally resents you."

That quick refocus caught me off guard. "What do you mean, personally resents me?"

"I don't know. I can only follow her thoughts as she has them, and her mind is rather scattered. I sense in the woman—"

"Meryl," I said helpfully. "Her name is Meryl Hawkins."

"Meryl. Meryl Hawkins seems to thrive on instant gratification. She is unable to tolerate any frustration of her desires. Her mind has a tendency to flare, briefly, to rage." Rex's forehead furrowed. "If you'd asked me whether these two people belong together, I would never believe they had any kind of relationship. They are incredibly different."

I stared at him. "You got all that in ten minutes?"

"I'm efficient." Rex inclined his head in the passenger seat as he returned my stare. I wasn't telepathic, but it seemed there was a story behind his efficiency he didn't want to tell. "Let's narrow down hard facts. You suspect the man might be behind the threat on Alice's life?"

"I do. In fact, he's the most logical suspect. He's already been arrested, and he has the most to gain if Alice dies," I explained. "Maybe he wants her dead because he embezzled and is about to get caught. Maybe she makes it more likely the company will hand over the evidence. Maybe he wants to be in sole control to keep that evidence from being handed over." I shrugged. "Maybe he just wants all the money and all the control. Maybe he initially killed her parents because he was playing a long game, and this is just the final phase." I shrugged again. "But yeah, he's the most obvious suspect."

"Or he was until the pixies jumped into this," Rex pointed out. "And the litany of maybes? Not hard facts."

"Maybe he's working with the pixies." Rex's expression turned doubtful as I tossed another maybe on the pile. "What? You said you can only follow what he's actively thinking of. Maybe he's not actively thinking of the plot while making out with a woman twenty years his junior. You don't know." I leaned forward and glanced up to the third floor. "What I know is we can't sit here all night eavesdropping." We needed to go talk to Pistachio Waterflash.

"You want to go confront the male pixie?" Rex asked.

My eyes narrowed. Another of my military-issued uniform benefits—aside from comfort, moisture-wicking, and making my waist look tiny—was certain innate defenses woven into the very fabric itself.

One defense was supposed to be blocking vampire telepathy.

"How did you know that?" I asked uneasily.

"I can't read your mind. If that's what you're asking."

"I didn't ask you that, did I?" I snapped. "I asked how you knew that." Way to go, Astra. You didn't sound defensive when you said that at all.

"I didn't know it. I suspected it. Hence, I asked a question and didn't make a statement," the vampire responded, his face a mask of expressionless mystery. "You have nothing to fear from me."

I nodded and reached for the keys to start the Jeep.

"That pixie chieftain on the other hand," he

murmured, gazing out the window, "enjoys no such immunity."

BACK AT THE SWAMP.

This time in the middle of the night.

You know what's most active between dusk and dawn in the miasma of stinky, sticky heat in the swamps of Florida?

Alligators.

In fact, it's estimated there's one alligator for every ten to fifteen people living in this steamy state. This ratio makes it just about impossible for someone living in Florida not to encounter an alligator at some point. It's like living in Jurassic Park with shopping malls.

Something you will never hear in Florida on a date?

Let's walk along the water's edge.

At night, the fresh waters of Florida come alive with sounds—and you don't necessarily know what's making those sounds. That splash could be a turtle slipping into the water or an alligator rising out of it. Maybe a snake swimming directly toward you. That tiny whoosh of the wind you felt on your cheek? It could be a fly, or it could be a bat.

During the day, swamps were challenging to navigate.

At night, they were treacherous. Everything was wet, slippery. Muddy or wrapped in algae. It was difficult to see five feet in front of you, impossible to feel your way through when everything felt the same.

Damp. Wet. Gross. Threatening.

Dangerous.

"I'd be happy to carry you," Rex offered quietly, a tinge of amusement on the edge of his words.

"That is so not gonna happen, vamp," I told him and then grunted as I slipped. "I can make it through here just fine." I wanted to kick myself for not grabbing a bottle of Althea's "Cat's Eye" potion before leaving the house.

How hard would it have been just to ask for the vial?

Not hard. Not hard at all.

More manageable than pulling my boot out of five inches of sucking mud.

I got my boot loose and picked my way forward, cursing my own foolishness. Aunt Gwennie was right. I did not, by default, think of my sisters for assistance or preparation. Thanks to that, I was quite literally groping through the darkness in an alligator-filled swamp.

How's that for a metaphor?

I slipped again and cursed loudly.

"Astra, I can see in the dark. You, clearly, cannot. I'd like to claim the offer to carry you is meant to simply be charming and chivalrous, but it's really out of concern for you," the vampire told me evenly. "That uneven rock you're stepping on?"

I froze. "Yes?"

"It's an alligator snapping turtle. A rather large one, I might add. And he seems a bit annoyed at present."

"Well, Rex, is it an alligator or a freaking snapping turtle?" I wiped the sweat from my brow. Reaching behind me, I hoped to find a tree to steady myself on so I could remove my foot from whatever life form I was unintentionally attacking. As my hand flailed, a cold hand grasped mine.

"It's a turtle. Alligator snapping turtle, a species of freshwater turtle," Rex said as if he were a middle school teacher leading a science field trip. "Lean on me and go backward," Rex breathed. "That's it. Use my hand for support to pull and just push back with your leg. I've got you."

I didn't really have a choice.

I couldn't see a thing.

I followed his directions, pushed, and slammed into Rex with a dull thud. His arms wrapped around me quickly and lifted me up. "Yeah, I don't need to be carried like some princess in a fairytale," I protested, pushing against him. "Put me down. I can do this."

"I'm not carrying you to protect you," Rex responded. He took wide strides north quickly enough that the wind blew through my short hair. "I'm protecting all the alligator snapping turtles. They were over-harvested in the seventies, you know, so now they're protected in Florida. I don't want you splitting their shells with your boot as you stomp through."

"I was not stomping." I sniffed. "How do you know so much about Florida wildlife?"

"I grew up here. So did you. The better question might be how you don't know."

Insulting.

"Go that direction." I pointed. "That's where Emma and I—" Remembering that first encounter with Pistachio, his words played once again in my mind. "He mentioned Ebony.

Pistachio Waterflash mentioned Ebony, but Ebony was with the rebel pixies." I frowned. "Whose side is she on?"

"Who's Ebony?"

I frowned. "You know, this was all a lot easier when we could just imprison people for interacting with humans as an out paranormal. I could've had this guy in a cell in Impy in a day. Since he's seven inches tall, it wouldn't have taken up much room. I could've transported him in an enchanted shoe box."

"Miss the old authoritarian regime, do we?" Rex asked, sounding amused.

"Come on, you have to admit acting with impunity is certainly easier. I could have had you arrested for carrying me like a sack of oatmeal." I snapped. "Just like that."

"You're heavier than a sack of oatmeal," Rex informed me.

"Rude."

Suddenly we slammed into a tree. Or what felt like a tree. I flew out of Rex's arms and rolled into the sticky mud. The vampire must've gone flying, but he reoriented himself so quickly that I was back in his arms before the fading momentum brought me to a halt.

"Now you brought a vampire into my

swamp?" a stern male voice, incensed, shouted at me. My eyes scanned the darkness, but I could see nothing. "Are you completely out of your mind? First, you bring a murderous owl, and now a vampire. What's next? Did you bury a kraken egg somewhere?"

REX HELD me tight in his arms as Pistachio Waterflash ranted and raved.

"Is he alone?" I whispered, frustrated I couldn't see.

"He appears to be," Rex whispered back.

I reached into my tool belt and pulled out a light stone.

Yes, I know what you're thinking. Why did I fumble my way through the swamp if I had a light stone tucked in my belt?

Well, first, I didn't want to announce our exact location even if the pixies were likely aware of our presence in their territory. Second, alligators have sharp above-water vision, and I didn't feel like giving them a bull's-eye.

I like my hand, thanks.

Pistachio could encourage the alligators to converge on our position and attack Rex and me if he felt like it. Whatever else was going on, this swamp was still pixie territory, and he was still the chieftain. My inability to see was now more of a hindrance than the target I would give the gators.

Just to be safe, though, I tossed it a body length away between Waterflash and me.

I'm not stupid.

The rock glowed white-pink, and the pixie's green hair flared brightly in the darkness. "Are you trying to challenge my authority here? I told you once. You're not welcome here. You're certainly not welcome here dragging a vampire behind you." Pistachio roared. I noted that his full-size body had expanded. Hence, he was slightly taller than Rex—even though he hadn't been in our previous encounter.

"I don't care about your authority, the pixies, or anything other than Emma and Alice right now." Rex gently lowered my feet to the ground so I could stand and deliver whatever speech was about to come while on my feet. He stayed so close. I could feel his body pressed against my back.

I didn't mind.

Alligators were fast.

Vampires were faster.

"Emma and Alice are fine. They're under my protection," Pistachio said, pulling his shoulders back like a king. "No harm will come to them."

"That's such bull. Emma and Alice are in my house, and you couldn't even get past the curb if you tried. So, chieftain, let's cut the crap." I crossed my arms. "Why have you drugged them? And why are they asleep?"

"They sleep during the night, obviously, because that's when female power is heightened." The pixie sighed with such pent-up frustration it was like my questions were the most he'd ever been put upon for anything in his entire life. "They follow me, a male pixie. Not the female pixies. It keeps them isolated from the extra female energy."

"So, what you're saying is that for women to continue to like you, you have to put them in a coma and isolate them from their women's intuition?" I asked him. His face cracked into a furious mask. "To tell you the truth, I could see that."

"I am Chieftain here!"

"You keep saying that," I nodded. I pointed to Rex. "Well, he's not chieftain. But he is Emma's brother, and Emma didn't choose to follow you.

So, out with it, pixie. Why did you forcefully drug a Forkbridge detective against her will?"

His face lost some of its lofty scorn. "But I didn't," he said, stepping back. For the first time, the arrogant pixie looked unsure of himself.

"I was here. I saw you touch her, and then she suddenly started thinking you were the best thing since sliced bread." I stepped forward. "Are you telling me you didn't sprinkle your stupid pixie dust crap on her?"

The harsh light of the rock painted the pixie's face in brightness and shadow. Pistachio suddenly looked fearful. "But I'm telling you the truth. I did nothing to Emma. You were here the entire time! I would never give anyone the dust without their consent," he told me, his eyes widening. "I couldn't!"

Rex leaned down. "He's telling the truth. Alice wanted the dust. He doesn't know what you're talking about with regards to Emma."

I stared at the pixie, breathing in the wet, heavy air. Unless Rex was part of this whole conspiracy, I had to trust what he said. But that... that made no sense.

Unless the rebel pixies were lying.

"And what about Meryl Hawkins?" I asked.

"She's simply a follower, Arden," Pistachio

responded. "A recent one, to be sure, but she, too, wanted to join the group."

Rex stepped around and faced me. "Meryl Hawkins was not asleep. It's the middle of the night. If he's telling the truth, and she's dusted, she should be asleep. If what he says is true, in any case."

I was having a heck of a time figuring out what was true and what wasn't.

I stood in the alligator-infested swamp facing an arrogant, misogynistic pixie. The powerful vampire at my side stared at me expectantly, his eyes dark with worry.

"How do you 'dust' your followers?" I asked, cringing a little at the question.

"They drink the sun elixir in the initiation ceremony," Pistachio responded. "The sun well water mixed with pixie dust. I add a little raspberry, strawberry, and mint, too, for flavor." He smiled, looking pleased with himself. "It's quite good."

"So they have to ingest it."

The pixie nodded.

"Is there some kind of magic spell you use to make the elixir control women?" I asked, remembering the rebel pixies' claim that Pistachio "somehow found a way" to create a concoction that gave him control over human women.

The pixie's face looked as confused as I felt. "No. This is our ancient pixie drink. Pixie dust and moon or sun water. We've been drinking it for hundreds of years." Pistachio looked back and forth between Rex and me. "I just shared a sip with the humans that wanted to walk the pixie path. Why?"

CHAPTER SIXTEEN

"So, I'm starting to feel like this civil war —wait, can we call it a civil war if there are only six pixies? Anyway, it seems to be a much bigger part of whatever is going on here than I first thought," I told Rex. "Everybody's story is just a little bit off."

After a brief glance at the pixie chieftain, Rex looked at me with that same intense but distant expression. "What do you mean?"

Instead of answering, I turned to Pistachio. "Earlier tonight, Ebony and Amethyst waylaid me with four other pixies. They took me to the moon pool and told me you had dusted four women to control them." I stared. "Is that true?"

Pistachio looked first angry, then guarded.

"I'm not going around searching out women to feed pixie water to, no. Alice sought us out. She came to me. You understand?" The pixie's tone was forceful, and he sounded frustrated—like he'd made this argument before. "She came into the swamp over and over again. For six months, maybe even a year, she kept visiting. I didn't go looking for her."

"Why? For what purpose?"

Suddenly, the pixie adopted a patronizing air. The switch in his attitude was so jarring, my head pulled back just a little in surprise. "Doing rituals to honor the pixies. Leaving us gifts." Pistachio shrugged. "She came so often, and with such dedication, I felt she earned a sip of the elixir. She wanted to follow a pixie path, but there was no pixie path." The pixie drew himself up to full height. "So, as is my right as chieftain, I created one. Though why I am explaining my choice to you, I have no idea."

Uh-huh.

My eyes narrowed.

"Did Ebony and Amethyst agree with your 'right' and your creation?" I asked him, glancing at Rex to see if his face held any outward indication that Pistachio was lying to us. As usual, it was a mask. "Did they have any problem with this new direction you went in as a leader?"

"I didn't ask them," he responded haughtily. "I am chieftain. They are not. I lead; they follow. That's how a pixie clan works. Why would I ask my subordinates for permission or input on what I, as a leader, already chose to do?"

"Wow. Yeah, okay. I'm sure the hostility in your voice didn't play a role in their discomfort at all." I rolled my eyes and did my best to stop openly scoffing at his offensive arrogance. I needed to keep him talking. "What about Emma? Why is Emma acting like she's dusted?"

"I have no idea. She hasn't come to this place for a year, leaving me gifts and flattering me," he responded with a dispassionate toss of his wild hair. "Though I wouldn't be averse to it if she was." He smiled with all the smugness I'd grown to expect from him. "The detective is quite a sexy little—"

"That is my sister you're speaking of." Rex's voice cracked like a whip. "Pixie blood is not my preferred libation of choice, but if you continue speaking of my sister in that manner? I will make an exception."

"Oh, just get out of my swamp, vamp!" The pixie rolled his eyes. "This is an ambush, and it circumvents my authority over the swamp." Fury flashed in his eyes. "Why do either of you care how many people I've given sips of pixie potion to? How is it the business of a witch and a vampire what I do?"

"Four people," I insisted again.

"One person!" he responded, incensed. "One person. Can you not count? One person. I gave Alice and Alice alone a sip of the pixie potion. What is the big deal about the stupid pixie potion, anyway? All it does is enable them to move through the swamp as someone who belongs here and make them a little more predisposed to adore the leader of the pixies. That's it. It's not dangerous."

"A little more predisposed?" I asked in a huff. " I have two women back at my house cooing over you like you're a member of the Beatles! At least they were until they both fell asleep."

"Beetles?" Waterflash blinked. "Are humans attracted to bugs?"

"Could you focus, please?"

Pistachio looked at me with an unspoken accusation, his face twisted in a wave of pained anger I just couldn't place. Then just as quickly, it disappeared.

There was something else going on here. I was sure of it.

And I was sure Pistachio Waterflash knew precisely what it was.

"Perhaps they just really like me," he said. "I am very likable."

Sure. You're all charm and good graces, bub.

I tried again.

"The owner of a multi-state grocery chain and a detective are acting like some nitwit high school girls with a crush on the quarterback. They don't just 'like' you. For one, you're not nearly as likable as you think you are. Two, their behavior seems out of control." Pistachio's arrogance broke into worry. "It's totally different from their normal personalities. You're the pixie, you tell me. How would that happen?"

The pixie looked at me, raising one eyebrow. "If the two women in your house are cooing over me, and you are sure they have been 'dusted,' it might mean they have taken too much of it. Much like alcohol, the pixie potion has standard —and safe—effects. But if a human takes too much of it? The effects come on too hard and too fast. It will wear off by morning. Or in a week." He tilted his head. "Maybe two."

"And who has access to this elixir?" Rex asked. "Who can make it?"

"Anybody," Pistachio said. "Well, any pixie. Pixie dust is kept on our two sacred well islands, and the alligators would ensure none but pixies and pixie guests went there. But it's a simple thing, like human Kool-Aid. You take some water, you put some pixie powder in it, you grab a spoon. Stir. Done. As I mentioned, I steeped mine in strawberry and—"

An image flashed in my mind.

"What color is it?" I asked, remembering the unlabeled plastic bottles filled with bright pink liquid on Emma's desk. "After you mix it together, what does it look like?"

"A sparkly pink, of course," Pistachio answered, looking insulted. "What other color could it possibly be? We're pixies."

I turned toward Rex. "When I came in for the newspaper interview this morning, Emma had a bunch of unlabeled bottles on her desk. Like, sports drink bottles? I think there were six of them," I said, trying to remember. "I don't know where she got them. I know they weren't from the vending machine at the police station." I raised an eyebrow. "What if this isn't Pistachio

Waterflash's fault? What if it's been Meryl Hawkins all along?"

"Hawkins?" Pistachio made a face like he'd bit into something sour. "That woman is the most insufferable—"

"How do you know her?" Rex asked, cutting Pistachio off before he could get rolling. The vampire's eyes quickly scanned the sky, marking the time, and then turned his attention back to the pixie. "Did she attempt to join the pixie cult?"

"It's not a cult," the pixie's fury flared. "It's one woman that likes me. I know someone like you couldn't understand—being a sexy vampire that can look at a woman sideways and flare attraction in her by blinking—but I resent your tone." Pistachio turned, his eyes clouded with concern. "I would never want to be the cause of any harm to Alice."

The pixie…seemed to blink back…tears.

I stared at him.

Yeah, those were tears.

Wait.

What?

Rex looked at me. I looked at him. We both looked back at the pixie chieftain. His arrogance struggled to hide the emotion he'd shown, to shield him from our intense stares…and failed.

The tiny pieces snapped into the puzzle as Pistachio's defenses fell away.

"You're in love with her," I said quietly, gently, and without judgment.

He looked down and blinked away pink pixie tears. "Leave me be."

"It's true, isn't it? That's it. You're in love with Alice Windrow."

And that is how we got the story—the true story— of the pixie "civil war."

"I DIDN'T INTEND to fall in love with a human," Pistachio began, gesturing towards three large, flat rocks. Rex and I seated ourselves and waited for the pixie to settle in and continue the story. "She was so lovely and so very...wounded." He leaned back and glanced out into the swamp. "She would come here several times a week, deep within the swamp, and meditate. At least once a week, she would speak out loud to the marsh as if it were alive and unload her burdens."

"About her parents?" I asked.

"About her parents, about the company she owned but didn't know what to do with. About her loneliness...she could no longer trust people because everyone seemed to want something. Alice was overwhelmed. And alone. So very alone." He smiled briefly, gently. "I think it's why she was drawn to the paranormal. The everyday reality wasn't giving her answers; it wasn't bringing her joy. Just crushing responsibility and black emptiness. I listened. For months, I listened." He swallowed. "Eventually, I appeared… to her."

"Does your kind have any rules about appearing to humans?" Rex asked.

Pistachio nodded. "Our clan avoids humans. My parents, the previous chieftains, felt it was better that way. We are small, can't easily change what we look like. And even when human-sized, we stand out. By our nature, we have flair," he told us breathlessly, holding his hands up and posing.

"I'd agree with you there," Rex told him.

His face fell, arms by his sides again. "I couldn't let her come to this place week after week and pour her heart out, hoping someone would hear, and let her leave thinking no one had. That she was still alone. I had to tell her that I heard her." He smiled. "That she was not alone."

"So you came up with the pixie path religion thing."

Pistachio nodded. "It was a way to give her some joy. And to stay near her. I did feel that it benefited my clan. Times have changed, and there are few wilds left humans do not encroach on. It was a compromise." He looked down. "It was also selfish. I couldn't stay away from her."

My eyes narrowed. "And the elixir to control her? Why did you do that?"

The pixie looked down, his face miserable.

"Pistachio?"

His brightly colored hair fell in front of his face, and he silently shook his head.

"She's in love with him as well," Rex told me quietly. "He knows they can never be together. He has to lead his clan, and they would never accept her as his mate. Pistachio felt guilty about starting something that led to even more pain for her, so he gave her the elixir to...turn her feelings. Instead of romantic love, she simply worships him like a god."

"There is an enforced distance to worship," Waterflash explained. "It was the only thing I had in my power to do besides abandoning her. And I couldn't do that. But I could protect her from the pain of being in love with someone she could never be with."

"And what about you?" I asked quietly. "What about your pain?"

The pixie shrugged. "It's of no consequence. It's also my own fault." He smiled sadly. "I knew the rules of my clan. I broke them. In doing so, I broke many things as well. Alice's ability to have a relationship with someone else. My own betrothal to Amethyst—"

Wait.

What?

"Wait a minute, wait a minute," I held my hands up in front of me. "You and Amethyst were going to get married?" Pistachio nodded. "So that means she was going to be a chieftain." He nodded again. "You broke off the engagement because you are in love with Alice? And told her exactly that?"

"Of course. I can't marry somebody when I am in love with another. That would be wrong. I owed her the truth." His eyes widened. "It's offensive to even suggest otherwise. I am surprised at you, witch, that you would even ask the question." He sniffed, looked insulted.

So, the pixies could drug people, block their natural emotions, lie—but marrying someone when in love with someone else?

That was an ethical bridge too far.

I sighed.

Pixies.

"How did she take it?"

"Not well," Pistachio admitted. "Amethyst believes her destiny as chieftain was not an accident of birth, but ratification of life's intended hierarchies. Pixies can be a bit snobbish. Especially toward humans."

Life's intended hierarchies?

That struck me as more than a "bit" snobbish.

"So not only did he spurn Amethyst—"

Pistachio interrupted Rex. "I wouldn't say spurned."

Rex looked at him sharply. "What would she say?"

The pixie didn't have an answer.

"As I was saying, he spurned Amethyst, robbed her of her leadership position when he refused and rejected her," Rex murmured. "It seems the list of suspects who would like to get revenge on Alice Windrow has just shortened. Considerably."

"Do you know anything about the Punktex grocery store being built in pixie territory?" I asked Pistachio.

He nodded. "I gave Alice permission to build the store on our land so she and I could have someplace to meet away from prying eyes. A couple of months ago, Amethyst came upon the two of us talking, and she was enraged. I needed somewhere safe where our meeting wouldn't cause pain." His eyes clouded with pain. But then they suddenly brightened. "We also absolutely adore chocolate. It's always risky for us to try and run into town to buy it, so Alice has been bringing it—but by the time she gets into the swamp, it's half-melted."

"The offerings Alice brings you?"

Pistachio nodded. "Chocolate, for the clan." Then he shuddered. "That chocolate is the only reason I haven't been removed as chieftain. Amethyst wanted me dethroned for consorting with the human. So long as the chocolate comes in, though, I remain chieftain." He held up his hands. "The grocery store on our land accomplished two things I needed to be accomplished."

If you knew pixies, what Pistachio Waterflash said makes perfect sense. Pixies don't like leaving their territory. They are addicted to chocolate the way a little kid is addicted to getting dirty. If pixies ate only chocolate all day, every day for the rest of their lives, they would die happy.

There's one thing pixies like more than chocolate, though.

Revenge.

Pistachio provided us with excellent reasons to sabotage a building site.

If you were Amethyst Cloudspirit, anyway.

I looked at Rex. "He's telling the truth?"

"He is." My vampire lie detector nodded.

"So, we've uncovered what's going on with the pixies, then," I said, stretching my arms. "But we haven't figured out how Meryl Hawkins fits into this." I raised my eyebrow. "Those pink drinks on Emma's desk, those had to be from Meryl Hawkins. A pixie slipping into the police department would definitely be noticed. But no one said a thing."

"Who else can make the pixie drinks again?" Rex asked.

"Anyone." He shrugged. "Like I said, we've been drinking them for years."

WITH ME BACK IN the vampire's arms, we left Pistachio Waterflash contemplating his actions and how they put everything he loved at risk. Rex clutched me close as we headed toward the moon pool. I'd worry about the alligators when we got there.

Meanwhile, my mind raced in so many directions.

Different paranormals despising other sentient beings.

Bigotry.

Intolerance.

Thousands of years, and we still hadn't stopped it.

This entire situation unfolding because a man and a woman…fell in love?

Well, that wasn't entirely true.

Their ill-fated romantic feelings (thanks to bigotry) might be the catalyst for this whole situation. Still, Pistachio Waterflash wasn't the one running around drugging women—despite the rebel pixies assertions.

If he had any faults—besides being super annoying—it was that he couldn't see past his own power and leadership to find the solution that was staring him right in the face.

Step down, dude. Just step down as chieftain, and go make a life with the woman you love. How hard is that?

"This way?" Rex asked, interrupting my internal rant.

I scanned the blackness. "How would I know? I can't see anything anymore."

The vampire grunted and continued moving east.

Before we'd left in search of the moon pool and the rebel pixies, Pistachio had shared one more tidbit of information.

Meryl Hawkins showed up in the swamp about six months ago with a folder full of notes on pixie magic. She wanted to do an exposé on the paranormals that lived among the humans in Central Florida, and Pistachio had all but run her out of the swamp on a rail.

So, Meryl Hawkins knew about pixies.

How much did she know about pixies?

Enough to work with a rebel group of them?

And to what end?

CHAPTER SEVENTEEN

It'd been a frightfully long night following a ridiculously long day, and I was tired. I'd started the day before at dawn's first light, and by my calculation, we were coming around to it again in just a few hours. I hadn't had so much as a nap.

"Do you want to rest?" Rex asked, slowing his stride. "You're beginning to look tired." The vampire's tone sounded concerned. "I can find a place for us to sit for a few moments if you'd like to close your eyes."

"You're doing all the work here, Rex, so if I wanted to close my eyes right now, I guess I could do it. No need for you to stop. But I'm fine." I yawned, rubbing my eyes with the heels of my palms. "I'm just mentally running through what the pixies told me the last time I was in the swamp. Ugh, this swamp," I snorted. "You know, I've been here three times in twenty-four hours. Maybe I should buy a condo."

"I'd hate to think of the shenanigans that would ensue if humans built a condo building in pixie territory." Rex's grip was firm as he carried me through the darkness. "I am curious. Did you not believe Pistachio Waterflash the first time you met him?"

"That pixie chieftain that we just met? The one just trying to protect the woman he loves? That guy is not who Emma and I met this morning. That wingnut seemed to go out of his way to be obnoxious and offensive." I sighed. "I don't know. If what he says it's true, I can't blame him for the lack of trust. Six pixie women trying to knock him off his throne? And they're threatening Alice's safety?" I shrugged. "He didn't know who we were. And my owl did try to eat him."

"He didn't say they threatened Alice," Rex said.

"No, but you haven't had the pleasure of meeting Amethyst Cloudspirit." I thought back to my meeting with the rebel pixies. They were working on getting us to side with them against

Pistachio Waterflash, but the two main pixies that spoke used very different tactics. While Ebony sought to charm us, Amethyst seemed to teeter on the edge of resentful aggression. "It's also clear the rebel pixies don't have the support of the wider pixie clan. Well, if Pistachio is right and chocolate works as a leadership bribe."

"If the clan didn't approve of his leadership, he wouldn't be leader anymore," Rex agreed. "That means that the rebel pixies are trying to perpetrate a coup." Rex's motion stopped, and he cradled me close as he leaned over slightly. "I think we're on the edge of the pond you spoke of."

I looked ahead of us. Tiny, itty-bitty flames flickered from the crevices and rocks across the water. It looked vaguely like the island. "That might be it. They had little tiny torches all over the place." I looked up at him. "Rex?"

"Yes?" he asked distractedly, still scanning ahead.

"You want to put me back on my feet there, buddy?"

His arms flexed with a hard tension. "I'm going to need to carry you over to that island. If that's where you intend for us to go."

"Probably. Can you tell if that's where the rebel pixies are?" I asked Rex.

"No," came a sharp voice from the darkness. "No, invaders, the rebel pixies are not on the sacred island. They are right here." A light flared, illuminating Amethyst's angry face. " Drop the witch, vampire."

"ARE YOU SHAKING?" Amethyst sneered.

Um. No. But I didn't answer.

"You should be. How dare you come back into our swamp dragging a vampire? That's twice in one day you've invaded our territory." I felt the pressure of her hand on my arm. "I have lost my patience with you, witch!"

"Have you now?" I tolerated the invasion of my space and the presumptuous grabbing of my arm without punching her in the face in hopes she would keep talking. Rex, standing behind me, followed my lead and said nothing. "And what patience have you been extending to me that has now run out?"

Then I yawned.

I honestly didn't mean to—it really had been

an incredibly long day, and I was exhausted. The pixie's expression was offended.

"We know that you just met with Pistachio Waterflash, and we know that you left him standing. Alive. You didn't attack him. After all that we told you, after all that we trusted you with—how could you give him the time of day? Whose side are you on?" She dropped her grip on my arm and turned to the pixie next to her. "I told Ebony that this witch would be of no use to us."

I wasn't shaking.

But I was intrigued.

What use did they think they would make of me? My eyes narrowed. Was Emma's "dusting" less about Emma and more about manipulating me into the position these pixies wanted me in?

"I'm on Emma's side. And Alice's side. I can tell you whose side I am not on." I crossed my arms. "I am not on Meryl Hawkins's side, and if you're working with her? You and I have a problem."

Amethyst was flanked by two pixies I didn't recognize—they were not at the island meeting earlier. At the mention of Meryl's name, they both jerked back slightly in surprise. Amethyst, of course, didn't look surprised at the mention of the reporter at all.

Interesting.

"Why would I be working with the human Pistachio drugged?" Amethyst glanced back at the two women as if ensuring they were still there. "I have no reason to have any discussions with that woman or any of the other three—"

"She's lying," the vampire interrupted. "And more than that, the two pixies behind her have seen her with the reporter multiple times," Rex murmured. "This one is lying to so many people she's having trouble keeping her own story straight in her head. She forgot these two have seen her with Meryl."

Amethyst's staff shot out toward Rex, and just as quickly, my arm blocked her attack. "None of that, Miss Saltypants. That's Emma's brother. If you want to start up a fight with the older brother of a Forkbridge detective you may (or may not) have caused some harm to, I suppose I can't stop you. But honestly," I said with a raised eyebrow, "is that really the way you want to play this?"

"I don't know what you're talking about," she replied in a flat voice

"Pistachio told us that the two of you used to

be engaged. He also told us that you felt pretty much entitled to lead the pixie clan, and his decision not to marry you put the kibosh on those plans. True?"

Her face twisted in anger.

"What?" One pixie's expression turned to one of scornful disbelief. "Amethyst, I thought you chose not to marry Pistachio because he was a misogynist that didn't respect women." The raven-haired pixie lowered her staff. "Is what the witch says true? Did you call off the engagement, or did he?"

Sweat suddenly beaded on Amethyst's forehead. "Don't listen to the witch! She's lying! They just don't want pixies to have any power here in Forkbridge! They're trying to divide us. Do you see why I have done what I've done?"

The other pixie lowered her staff slightly and looked confused.

"The witch is not lying," Rex told them both. "You both know vampires can read minds, correct?" They nodded with frowns, their eyes wary. "I heard Pistachio Waterflash's story, and unless there is some new magic I am unaware of? Your chieftain was not lying to us when he said he told Amethyst he could not marry her because he loved another."

"He said what?" The raven-haired pixie's eyes grew even wider. "Amethyst?"

"The vampire is a liar!" Amethyst's face twisted with rage.

"Your illustrious leader here has been meeting with Meryl Hawkins?" I asked them. "We just caught Meryl Hawkins in an office with Paul Wakefield, the married CEO of Punktex. She's having an affair with him, which seems a little weird since Amethyst claimed earlier Meryl is one of Pistachio's drugged, devoted cult women —even though Pistachio says he hasn't been going around drugging women and has no cult."

Amethyst looked gobsmacked, her eyes moving back and forth between us.

There was a breathless hush as the two pixies considered my words.

"You confirmed that with your powers, vampire?" the smaller of the two asked, her face concerned. "You confirmed that Pistachio has not been going around drugging women? That this is a…lie?"

Rex raised his eyebrow. "I did."

"Are you going to believe a vampire and a witch over me?" Amethyst hissed at them. "How dare the two of you even open your mouths when I am around! I am the leader here, not you! You're simply here to serve me! Now, keep your mouths shut! I command that both of you maintain silence for the remainder of this encounter!"

If Amethyst expected the two women to cower in fear, she didn't get the response she was looking for. They stared back at her, angry.

"Wow. Someone skipped right over the positive leadership course in pixie school, I see," I observed.

"You told us you dumped Pistachio. That you rejected him for his crimes!" the raven-haired pixie said, throwing down her staff. "You told us that he was drugging human women! That he was abusing them! Why would you lie about such a thing?"

Amethyst, momentarily taken aback, turned to face her.

"And you claimed that Punktex would belong to the pixies in just a few months," the other added, her anger quiet but no less intense. "Suddenly, the victim Meryl you claim to have been helping is having an affair with its CEO? What have you done? What have you made us a party to—without our consent?"

Amethyst looked indignant. "I don't have to explain myself to you. It's ridiculous that you think I should have to," she said dismissively.

"You are not chieftain, Amethyst Cloudspirit! I demand that you tell us what's going on. Clearly, you've been lying to us, your sisters, for months now." The angry pixie waited for a response, but Cloudspirit simply stared at her in stony silence. "That is not the sign of a leader. You're no leader."

"I am—"

"I follow you no more." The quiet purple-haired pixie broke her staff over her knee and threw it at Amethyst's feet. "No wonder Pistachio did not want you."

The former pixie leader's face twisted in rage.

I blinked.

I knew pixies could be capricious and flighty, but I didn't expect the two pixies flanking Amethyst to turn on her so quickly. And not based on the word of a vampire. Or a witch.

"Why do you believe us over her?" I asked.

"She lied to you about Meryl Hawkins," one of them stated. "I know this the same as I know my own name or the waters of this swamp. I have seen them together. What's more, I heard her...lie to our seer about the Hawkins woman." She looked mortified. "How did I not see this? How did I ignore these little offenses for so long?"

"Little offense?" the other asked. "It is the

highest offense in our clan to lie to the seer. Nutmeg, why did you not say something?"

"I believed!" Nutmeg said with a shake of her head. "She is my sister!"

"Oh, that's just rich. You believe a vampire and a witch over me? Over me? Nutmeg, Windsong— how can you betray me like that?" Amethyst looked enraged. Her eyes skittered in multiple directions as if she was watching her plan shatter into pieces like an expensive vase. The two women facing her down looked more than a little miffed themselves. "I am a warrior of the pixie clan. Everything I do is for Clan Waterflash—"

"That's right, Clan Waterflash, not Clan Cloudspirit!" Windsong shouted. "I have seen you with Meryl Hawkins! You claimed to be helping her. You claimed to be freeing her from Pistachio's grip, and yet here we find that she is tempting Paul Wakefield to break his oaths to his wife!" The lithe pixie stomped her foot. "If she were truly drugged by Pistachio, if they shared the elixir? She would not be engaging in such actions!"

"To tempt men to betray their wives for no reason? This is not the pixie way!" Nutmeg added, her tiny nose judgmentally in the air.

I yawned again.

"Are we keeping you up?" Amethyst hissed.

"Sorry. I'm usually asleep at night." I looked around. "So what now?"

"We will tell Ebony of this one's crimes of dishonesty," Nutmeg said, pointing an accusatory finger at Amethyst. "It would not surprise me if she were banished from the swamp and—"

"Banish me? Like I even want to be here! I was doing all this for the clan, but you ungracious pixie twits don't deserve what I was going to do for you, anyway!" Amethyst roared. The warrioress struck toward Nutmeg with her staff, and I jumped forward again to block it. "We were going to leave this godforsaken pit of mosquitos and alligators! All of us! We were going to live like kings! With refrigerators for the chocolate!" She stepped backward. "Stay here and rot in the heat, then, for all I care! Peasants!"

Amethyst turned and ran into the dark swamp.

REX MOVED TO SPEAK, but I held my hand up.

"Can you track her?" I asked him, pointing. "I want to follow her, but I want to talk to them first."

"I can, yes," Rex said, studying me with his cold, discerning eyes. "But I want to—"

"Them first." I pointed, turning toward the pixies. "I'm so sorry to have brought this to you in this way," I told them.

"I appreciate it, witch. I can't say I thank you for this information," Nutmeg told me sadly. She glanced at the shadowed brush where her former leader, Amethyst, had disappeared. "My heart grieves for the loss of my sister, though it rejoices for the return of our honor."

"Yes, our honor is the most important thing," Windsong agreed.

"Well, I'm glad for that. I did want to ask, though—did you happen to overhear what Amethyst and Meryl Hawkins were talking about?" Rex moved to speak again, but I waved him quiet. "Just give me a sec. They have to get going."

Rex closed his mouth and leaned back, waiting quietly.

"They were talking about someone going to jail," Windsong explained. "I thought they were helping someone named Alice to get back what was rightfully hers, but now?" The pixie looked perplexed. "Now, knowing what I know, I am not sure what Amethyst's plan was. If she lied about the humans being abused, what else did she lie about?"

And suddenly, it all clicked.

Well, maybe.

"Huh. What if Paul Wakefield didn't embezzle any money at all?" I said to Rex. "What if this was some long-game con by Amethyst and Meryl?" Amethyst's parting shot that the pixie clan would've gotten out of the swamp to live like kings echoed in my mind. My jaw dropped. "What if this is all about money? Revenge and money? Maybe Meryl and Amethyst were like Bonnie and...um, Bonnie."

Rex frowned. "The problem is—"

"No, wait, hear me out. If Paul Wakefield goes to prison for embezzlement, all the control reverts back to Alice, right?" I explained to him. "But if he doesn't go to prison for embezzlement, and Alice dies, all the control and money goes to him. By having control of both of them? Amethyst and Meryl cover all their bases." I held up my hands. "The pixies have an elixir that makes someone worship them. Control them, right? So presumably, whatever they tell them to do? They'll do."

Rex sighed. "It's an interesting hypothesis, but—"

"I know." I nodded, assuming he spotted the same hole I did. "But the elixir made Emma and Alice worship the chieftain of the pixie clan. How would that help Meryl and Amethyst?" I frowned. "Amethyst seems to hate him."

"That's not necessarily how it works," Nutmeg interrupted.

I turned. "What do you mean? How what works?"

"The elixir is used in marriage ceremonies, at births. The elixir bonds more deeply two people that have the beginnings of a new bond. Understand? Or, well, it can. The effect fades after a time, but for a few days? The potion cements total loyalty between two people that have started down a path."

"Between two people?" I raised my eyebrow.

"Well, yes, two people take it at the same time, of course," Windsong said. "You wouldn't want just one person to take it. Whoever they took it in the presence of? They would be under the control of…that person…oh, I see what you mean." The pixie chewed her lip nervously. "That's not how it's supposed to be used at all."

"But, wait a minute—Emma drank the elixir while she was with me." I frowned. "Why did she have a huge crush on Pistachio instead of me, then?"

"She is not bisexual," Nutmeg shrugged. "Or if she is, she's simply not that into you. You're quite attractive and all, but you can be a little abrasive at times. I can see that being a problem."

"Oh, yes, that's likely why," Windsong added.

Rex chuckled. I glared at him. "So it's a romantic thing?"

The pixie held up her fingers and listed all the ways the elixir could be used. "Romantic, familial, or religious, yes," Windsong said.

I rolled my eyes. "All this magic has such specificity it just drives me nuts. Okay, so you can use it with two people or just one person. Family, romantic, or religious bonds—but not friendships or two people with no ties. Wait a minute—if one person takes it alone, how do they get controlled?"

"I don't understand," Nutmeg said.

"Like, if I took some right now and no one else did, who would control me? Rex because he's closest? You because you're a pixie?"

"Oh, me," Windsong said, raising her hand. "I had some a few hours ago. Nutmeg had some yesterday. I would eclipse the pull of any other relationship because I drank the potion most recently."

"So, whoever had the drink most recently?"

Windsong nodded.

"This is enough to give me a headache," I muttered.

"I don't think we need to deep dive into the intricacies of pixie magic," Rex said with another shrug. "It's clear from Amethyst's own words what she was planning, or at least her end goal—money, taking over the pixies as the leader, pushing Pistachio out. My main concern is my sister. Can we reverse the hold this elixir has on them?"

"Oh, sure." Nutmeg nodded. "Just give them water from the opposite well."

"I got it!" Archie shouted from the trees above us. "I'll go get it! I'll be right back!"

"Be back?" Rex looked up. "That owl certainly is quiet." Looking down, he tilted his head. "Which well is the opposite well? Is it from the men's well or the women's well? Aren't they completely different?"

"Totally different." Nutmeg nodded.

"Not even remotely different other than location. They're springs," Windsong snorted and glanced at the other pixie. "They're both pulling

up water from the same underground aquifer."
She smiled at me. "Just give them water from the
spring without pixie dust. They'll be fine."

"That's blasphemy!" Nutmeg told the other
pixie.

"Maybe. Still true." Windsong shrugged.

Nutmeg's eyes went wide and she gave a
strangled little squeak.

"Now that we've settled that, I have one tiny
wrench to throw in your well-thought-out
conclusion, Astra," Rex said, turning. "It's a small
one. Just a small point."

"Oh?"

"Amethyst Cloudspirit had no idea Meryl
Hawkins and Paul Wakefield were having an
affair. None. She was as surprised as Nutmeg and
Windsong," Rex said. "Maybe even more."

"Why didn't you say something earlier?" I
asked, frustrated.

He paused for a moment, staring at me.

Then the vampire threw his head back and
laughed.

"What the heck is so funny?"

Rex tried to say something, but he started
laughing again. I was starting to think that he was
having some kind of weird vampire seizure when

he caught his breath and wiped the tears from his eyes.

"What is wrong with you?" I asked, thunderstruck at his reaction.

"I'm sorry," he said, finally getting a hold of himself. "I shouldn't laugh. You've been busy. It's nothing." Waving a hand, the vampire gestured toward Nutmeg and Windsong—who were now snickering.

"He's right. Totally nothing," Windsong agreed.

Despite my utter lack of comprehension regarding what the heck was so funny, Rex's laughter was kind of contagious, and I smiled in spite of myself. "Really. Come on, tell me," I asked again, my tone friendly. "What's nothing?"

"It's nothing. I promise," he said, wiping red-tinged tears from his eyes.

"You don't want to know, anyway," Nutmeg explained.

"Yes, because we're laughing at you." Windsong nodded. "So it's probably better we don't tell you."

Rex burst into a fresh round of laughter.

CHAPTER EIGHTEEN

*A*fter the pixies and the vampire finished laughing at me, Rex and I took off after Amethyst Cloudspirit. The indignant pixie, according to Rex, was mono-focused on one thing—finding Meryl Hawkins. It didn't take us long to catch up with the sprite on the edge of the swamp. Eventually, after a short trip, me in the vampire's arms, we found her pacing a remote stretch of road.

"Stupid woman thinks she can make a fool out of me," Amethyst muttered. Her arms dangled at her sides as she moved, eyes wide and searching. Every so often, the pixie tensed, her hands clenching, and her knuckles turning white.

"She keeps looking in that direction," I

whispered to Rex. The two of us crouched low behind a boulder so large the Angel of Death would have mistaken it for his own oversized tombstone.

"I think she's waiting for Meryl," he whispered back.

We stayed there, quiet. Only the sounds of crickets and the hooting of owls broke the silence. I glanced up. The hint of light in the clouds reminded me that Rex's help was getting close to expiring. "Do you have somewhere to sleep tomorrow?" I asked him.

He nodded. "Emma's place has a basement."

"Is it comfortable?" I asked. Rex stared at me with a strange look on his face. "Just making small talk."

He shrugged. "If you like damp stone walls, I suppose it's fine. Look." Rex pointed. "There's a car coming."

I looked out onto the street. A car drove up to the curb and stopped. Its headlights were off like it was trying to avoid being seen, but I could tell it was a large black SUV. The driver opened the car door with such a ferocious shove I could hear the metal complaining from my hiding spot.

"Are you out of your mind?" Meryl snapped at Amethyst before both feet were on the ground.

"Why would you call me? We shouldn't be seen together, and we certainly shouldn't have cell phone records tying the two of us. For a paranormal being, you're not the smartest tack in the box, are you?"

"Don't you talk to me that way!" Amethyst fumed. "There is no aspect of your plan that has worked the way you said it would. Not one! Alice is still alive. Pistachio is still the chieftain. She and that detective are in the witch's house surrounded by a gaggle of teen paranormals and the high priestess of a freaking war goddess! A war goddess, I might add, that decided at some point the person I want dead shouldn't die."

"Calm down, Amethyst," Meryl warned the pixie.

"Calm down? The most I've been able to do is shrink some fuel injectors, and what did that accomplish? Exactly nothing." The pixie stepped up to the reporter. "You're not the mastermind you think you are."

"Your stupid pixie elixir isn't the be-all-end-all of magical roofies that you claimed it was," Meryl spat back. The reporter leaned forward, shaking her finger in the pixie's face. "They were supposed to be controlled, not so ridiculously loopy that everyone knew something was wrong! How did you think that was going to work?"

"I didn't tell you to pour a gallon down the police woman's throat!" The pixie had an angry light in her eyes, so angry it practically glowed.

"Well, now we have a detective that's too drunk on pixie elixir to be controlled. Alice is loopy because she's next to the potion-soaked detective, so much so they know she's messed up, too—"

"The witch already spoke to Pistachio. She and that vampire probably know everything. Which is more than I knew two hours ago." The pixie pointed a finger at the reporter and fumed with an almost unimaginable intensity. "Why didn't you tell me you were having an affair with Paul Wakefield?"

Meryl rolled her eyes. "The vampire and witch probably know everything? And you want to talk about who I'm sleeping with. I swear, Amethyst, you're going to give my ulcers a workout." The reporter groaned, rubbing one of her fists to her temple. "Look, we can still salvage this. It'll just be a longer game, that's all. It may take us a few more months—"

"Months?" Amethyst's face twisted into fury, and then, all at once, she seemed to deflate. With an exasperated sigh, she covered her face with her hands. Removing them a second later, she glared at her companion. "If you think I'm going to continue to help you without getting the satisfaction that I deserve—especially since you are lying to me—you have another think coming," the pixie said dryly. "I signed up for this to unseat Pistachio, become the pixie chieftain, kill Alice Windrow for all she took from me, and to bring the pixies out of the swamp and into a luxurious condominium." She crossed her arms. "One of those things needs to happen tonight, or I will take my frustration out on you, human."

"It's not easy trying to take over a multi-million dollar corporation, you twit," Meryl responded arrogantly despite the apparent threat the pixie had just issued. "You may have magic water in your world, but in my world? Stealing millions of dollars and actually getting to keep it involves some planning. Finesse. Patience."

"You stole the money to blame Paul Wakefield easily enough." Amethyst turned and looked at Meryl's vehicle. "Nice SUV. An Escalade, no? What do those run these days?" Meryl's face remained impassive. "I may live in a swamp, but I'm not an idiot. You took it for yourself. I want my own satisfaction tonight, or this partnership ends."

Rex and I looked at each other. "Should we grab them?" he whispered. Before I could answer, Meryl responded.

"Fine. We can go by my house and pick up a knife that I took off of one of the cops at the station," Meryl told the pixie. "It should frame him well enough for the murder." She turned and walked toward her car. "Well, murders. We should kill the detective, as well, if she's in the same place as Alice. That will send the cops scrambling every which way. Especially after I write articles accusing them of corruption."

Amethyst looked dubious. "That home and those women are under the protection of the goddess Athena—"

"Stop being so superstitious. If the gods had any real power, we would've been stopped a long time ago. Get in." Meryl slid into the driver seat, and the pixie complied, quickly shutting the door behind her.

Rex's tension as they drove away was off the charts. I was impressed that he had any self-control whatsoever while listening to two women casually discuss murdering his sister. Once they were gone, we stood up.

"So, this was all about money and revenge."

"I got news for you, Rex. It's usually about money and revenge." I looked at Rex. "I assume we can get there way ahead of them if you take us?"

He nodded.

"Okay. I have an idea. Archie?" I called toward the tops of the trees. The owl had been quiet the whole time, but I knew, somehow, he was there. "You're here, right?"

"Here!" A voice called down from somewhere in the trees.

"Give us the water, and go tell Pistachio what's going on. Tell him not to go in the house until the lights are on. That's really important, Archie. Really, really important."

"Got it!"

The owl flew down and dropped two leather pouches of liquid from his talons. Without stopping to talk or make snarky comments, he launched off my arm and flew silently into the night.

I jumped into Rex's arms and explained my plan as we headed at breakneck speed to Arden House.

REX EFFORTLESSLY LEAPED toward my mother's window.

We just didn't have time to spare.

"Mom, I need you to wake up," I called as the two of us scrambled in her bedroom window. Once in, I tossed the water to Rex and pointed toward the hallway. "Let me know if it doesn't work." He nodded and took off toward Emma and Alice.

"What time is it?" she asked sleepily.

"Late. Or early. I don't know. It doesn't matter. Come on, get up. You, too, Aunt Gwennie." I raced over to my aunt's bed and shook her awake. "Get up. I need you guys to take down the wards. No, don't turn that light on!"

"Astra, have you lost your mind?" my mother asked huffily, her arm midway toward the lamp. Mom dropped her head back on her pillow. "It's the middle of the night. Now get back into your bed this instant. Your aunt and I will help you in the morning."

"I haven't been to bed yet," I told her. "Come on. Hurry."

A delicate snore escaped my mother's parted lips.

Oh, come on!

I raced toward her bed, then shook my

mother's shoulder, causing her to wake again with a start. In the darkness, I could see my aunt get out of her bed. "What is it, Astra?" Aunt Gwennie asked sleepily.

"Meryl and Amethyst, a pixie, are on their way over here to try and murder Alice and Emma. I need you to keep the lights off and hide and be quiet and let them try. After taking the wards down, I mean," I explained quickly.

"You need us to what now?" Aunt Gwennie stared at me. "Astra, darling, did you hit your head?"

"I need you to take down the wards so they can both get in. Since, you know, they actually intend harm for people in this house? Yeah, wards down." I looked at the two. "Like, right now. Chop chop." I stared. They stared back. "Now. I mean, like, right now."

My mother sat up. "Astra, you need to explain to us—"

"I can't. There is no time. I have no time to explain it to you. You're going to have to trust me." I glanced at the door. "I need to go warn my sisters, and tell them to hide upstairs and keep the lights off." My mother and I stared at one another. "Mom, please. Please. You have to trust me."

The pause seemed to go on forever, but it really didn't.

"Okay." She was still looking at me like I had my head turned backward, but she nodded. "We'll trust you, Astra. If the goddess trusts you to save Alice, we have to have faith. Your aunt and I will stay up here and take down the wards. It shouldn't take longer than a minute at most."

"I'll get the things we'll need," Aunt Gwennie said, gathering a couple of items from a cabinet next to her bed. I watched. Pausing, she turned to stare at me. "I know your mother agreeing to trust you is a momentous occasion in your life that you might like to mark with reflection, dear, but someone still needs to warn your sisters. We can take care of this."

"Oh, right, yeah. Sorry."

I found all three of my sisters in bed. I quickly explained what I needed from them—and warned them the wards would be down. Each nodded, held their questions, and raced into their closets to hide.

"Goddess, please keep them safe," I whispered as I raced down to the first floor. I paused on the last step, realizing I just asked a god I didn't believe in to protect my sisters.

I shrugged, jumping to the first floor.

No time to think about it now.

"Okay, upstairs secure," I told Rex. He sat on the coffee table in front of Emma and Alice.

"Astra, this is all, like, completely crazy," the detective told me. She sounded like herself and, lucky for us, awake and alert. "How did Rex even get here?" She turned and stared at her brother. Then she frowned. "You peeked, didn't you? I thought you and I had a talk about that. It's only supposed to be for emergencies."

"Are you off your rocker? What on earth would you call this?" the vampire asked her incredulously. "This isn't an emergency? I swear, Emma."

I suppressed a smile.

Rex, he of super-serious demeanor and inscrutable facial expression, sounded just like an exasperated non-vampire big brother frustrated with his little sister.

"I don't understand what's happening," Alice whispered. She looked back and forth between all of us, trying to parse out what she was doing here. "He's a vampire?"

"That's not important," I told her. "This is what's important. A reporter and a pixie are coming in here to kill you both. I need you both to pretend to be asleep on the couch. Rex and I will be right over there hiding." I pointed to a door. "Just before they do the deed, we're going to take them down. Then Emma will arrest Meryl, Pistachio can do whatever he wants with Amethyst—"

"Pistachio is here?" Alice looked around the room like a lovesick puppy.

"He will be. Guys, we have to hide. Is everyone clear on what's going to happen?" Everyone nodded. "Okay, let's all get in positions."

Emma and Alice appeared to wrap around each other on the couch in a sleepy pile of limbs. Still, I could tell that Emma had positioned herself so she could protect Alice from any attacks. Rex and I slipped ourselves into a space between the large herb cabinet and an open door. No one could spot us unless they went out of their way to look.

"Now we wait," he whispered.

I looked up at him. "Now we wait."

WE DIDN'T HAVE to wait long.

The two women picked the back door lock and slipped in with all the silent finesse of a pair of elephants. "Watch out, move out of the way!"

Amethyst hissed. "You're about as good at sneaking as a hippopotamus in high heels!" A flashlight scanned around the room. "On the couch! They're over there!"

The pair now crept forward carefully, as if they expected us to jump out and surprise them at any moment. When nothing happened, their stride sped up, and their voices became slightly louder.

"Hold the knife by the plastic bag," Meryl told Amethyst. "You don't want to get your fingerprints on it."

"Wait, me?" The pixie sounded surprised. "Why do I have to stab them?"

The sound of a blade sliding out of its sheath made me wince.

"Because I'm a human, dummy. My fingerprints are probably on file somewhere. Do you even have fingerprints? Besides, aren't you the one that wants her dead?" In the darkness of the living room, I could see the outline of Meryl holding out the blade to Amethyst. "You want her dead. You should stab her."

"Well, I don't want the cop dead. She didn't sleep with my fiancé," Amethyst said, her voice dripping with ice.

"I hear you. But I didn't want anyone dead,"

the reporter retorted. "I just wanted to be rich. You're the one that started talking about killing people. If you don't want to murder somebody, why did you even bring it up?"

"Oh, I have had just about enough of these two," Emma said, jumping up off the couch.

She launched herself upward, fist balled, and delivered an uppercut to Meryl's considerably-sized chin. Fist met face with a resounding crack, and Meryl staggered backward. Without drawing back for another punch, Emma slammed the bend of her arm into Amethyst's face in a perfectly executed elbow strike.

"Was that the plan?" Alice whispered, eyes wide.

"Probably not," Emma told her cheerfully. "But if I had to listen to one more statement from either of these two idiots, I would've had to kick them, and that just wouldn't have been as efficient."

I raced out to grab the pixie. Before I got two steps across the room, I blinked and discovered Rex already had her. "Get the lights," he told me. "I sense Pistachio out among the trees, and he's distraught."

"About me?" Amethyst asked hopefully.

"You really don't have a very firm grip on reality, do you?" Rex asked the pixie politely.

My mother and Aunt Gwennie raced down the stairs. "We saw the lights on. Is everyone all right?"

"Ms. A, did you doubt our ability to take down these two idiots?" Emma asked my mother, her tone pleased. "I got this one with one punch to the face, the other one with an elbow, and I was in a drugged coma for, like, a day. Oh, speaking of idiots." Emma reached behind her and pulled out a set of handcuffs.

Meryl's eyes grew wide. "What are you doing?"

Emma slapped the cuffs on the reporter's wrists. "You have the right to remain silent—"

"You can't arrest me! I'll tell everybody about this! I'll tell everybody about witches and pixies!" Meryl screeched, trying to pull away from Emma's grip. "I'll tell them all about the paranormal, and you'll all be exposed!"

"You can tell everybody all about the paranormal," Emma agreed. "You can tell the prosecutor about witches, about vampires, about pixies. You can tell them about the little tiny people that live in the swamp that can talk to alligators." Her head tilted to the side. "When you start telling people that don't believe in the paranormal about this stuff? Well, you just sound like a nutter. So, rock on. You do you."

"But it's true!" Meryl screamed. "I can expose you all!"

"You do your best, there, sweet cheeks," Emma told Meryl, shrugging. "My guess is all that's going to do is determine whether you go in a concrete cell or a padded one. People have been trying to use paranormal defenses since that 'devil made me do it' trial. No one gets off an attempted murder charge 'because pixies.' I mean, come on now. This is Florida. No one gets off for anything here." Emma tilted her head. "Well, except that Zimmerman guy. But that's a whole different discussion."

"You stupid idiot! You and your revenge fantasy!" Meryl spat at Amethyst. "This is all your fault!"

"How do you feel?" I asked Emma with concern.

"Man, that nap totally got me ready for this." Emma winked at me. "I have the best fun with you, Astra, I swear. I always wanted to try a punch like that. It's not often anyone comes at me from above. Did you see her fly back? Ha! How many people can say they delivered an elbow strike to a murderous pixie? Not many, I bet."

The back door slid open, and a brightly colored head tentatively peeked in. My mother welcomed him, and he nodded to her formally.

Alice gasped. "Pistachio!"

"Alice!" Pistachio ran in, his eyes seeking the human woman he wasn't supposed to love but did.

Alice smiled. Her eyes were red, and tears were running down her cheeks. The pixie chieftain ran to her, and Alice threw her arms around him, hugging him tightly and burying her face in his shoulder. "I'm so sorry," she whispered.

"It's okay," Pistachio said. He stroked her hair. "You have nothing to apologize for, nothing to be sorry for. This fiasco is my fault." Over Alice's head, he glanced at Amethyst. "I should have been honest with everyone. Maybe we could have avoided this. I'm just...I'm just glad you're all right."

We all smiled.

Well.

Not Amethyst.

Or Meryl.

Those two were pretty annoyed.

But everybody else.

CHAPTER NINETEEN

The runners sailed across the finish line.
Well, sailed may be generous.

First, speedy entrants sailed through with a wave to the cheering crowd. Then runners kind of…loped. Eventually, they came in exhausted clusters, covered with sweat, limping across the temporary white line painted across High Street.

Alice Windrow didn't care. She waited to shake every hand, give every participant an encouraging hug. The Alice Windrow who waited to shake everyone's hand was not the same one who had lain on the couch for a day or chased after the pixie chieftain with a lovesick fervor. This Alice stood firm, confident. She looked ready to shake hands with the entire world.

"Dad always waited, all the way to the end," she explained once there was a break in the competitors. "He praised every child, every adult: the runners, the volunteers. In the end, he made sure everyone knew they'd had an audience. That they were seen." Alice walked back to stand with me in the hot Florida sun. "I mean, we were just people that came to watch, right? But Dad loved these things." Her eyes grew watery. "I guess that's why I do it, now that I can."

"No one would know you were practically comatose a couple of days ago," I told her. "Everything came together beautifully. Looks like it went off without a hitch."

She looked around. "Yeah. Hey, let's go stand under that canopy. Looks like it will be a little while before the rest of the runners catch up." Alice glanced toward the sky. "The sun is just brutal."

I smiled.

That was likely the most common phrase uttered in Florida in the summer, especially in the afternoon.

Even so, I was enjoying the leisurely Sunday, standing under the trees around the Forkbridge

Community Center, watching the sweaty competitors in Alice's marathon cross the finish line. The air felt damp, and I could faintly detect the fresh salt in the breeze. The air in this park smelled like...home.

Technically, I was there to guard Alice's life, just in case we didn't get everyone who was involved in the conspiracy to murder her. In reality, though? It was just a formality.

Ami reported the star card stopped glowing, finally, sometime yesterday afternoon. We later realized it was just a few moments after Clan Waterflash formally banished Amethyst Cloudspirit from the swamp and surrounding areas.

Human justice would move more slowly, but apparently, the card understood that. Meryl Hawkins in a cell seemed enough to satisfy its need for justice.

Emma stepped out from the crowd and joined us in front of the Forkbridge Community Center. "Hey there!" she called cheerfully. Slipping beneath the shade of the canopy, she slapped Alice on the back. "Looks like a great turnout."

"More than we bargained for," said Alice. "The volunteers said there was a rush to sign up after Meryl Hawkins' arrest hit the papers. I guess

318 | LEANNE LEEDS

everyone has a morbid curiosity about crime, even though nothing really happened. As far as everyone knows, I was just in hiding for a day."

"Just think of how many people would sign up if they knew the real story," I joked. "Someday, the world will be ready to know about witches and pixies, I'm sure. But I'm also sure today is probably not that day. Look at how they already treat the spiritualists in Cassandra."

"It's not that bad, but it's not that good, either." Detective Sullivan nodded. "Awful about Amethyst Cloudspirit, but it appears justice has been done by pixie rules." She paused. "You know, I don't want to talk out of turn, but pixie justice leaves me a bit nervous about what it means for Forkbridge. Banishment seems like a way of washing their hands of the whole thing and making that psychotic pixie our problem. Their territory is just a small swamp."

"They banished her from the state," I explained to Emma.

"Oh?"

"Yeah, we don't have to worry about her in Forkbridge. Alabama and Georgia might want to be on alert, though."

"Clan Waterflash did what they had to do, I

suppose," Alice added. But she didn't look happy. "I just wish none of it had happened at all."

"This had been in the planning stages for a long time," Emma told her. "Cloudspirit came into this thing relatively late, but Meryl? She's been working on this plan since your parents died." Alice's eyes widened. "No, no. Your parents were not murdered—that accident really was an accident. But guess who was assigned to look into that for the *Gazette*?"

"Meryl," I guessed.

"You got it. She found out about all the intricacies of the trusts and holdings under the guise of investigating the accident."

"Then she used that to make a plan to steal it all," I told Alice.

Alice shuddered. "But how did she get involved with Amethyst and the pixies?"

"Long game, I guess," Emma said, shrugging. "She probably followed you, put two and two together about you and Pistachio. Maybe she overheard you guys when you met. Whatever it was, once she realized what was going on, she sought out Amethyst to use her, and the rest is history."

"That's just diabolical," Alice told the detective.

"She's not talking yet, but we found enough information at her house from the search warrant to put a lot of this together. Lucky for us, she takes meticulous notes."

"What do the other cops think about all the pixie stuff?" Alice asked.

"That she's nuts." Emma smiled. Then she shrugged. "I told her. But they think the people with the crazy names in her notes are either code or imaginary."

A very familiar smell, one of the sickly sweet scents of the pixies—a mixture of clove cigarettes and stale copper—hit me for just a moment. I looked around, scanning the crowd, but no shocks of vibrant hair jumped out at me.

"You okay?" Emma asked.

I turned and saw she was staring at me, concerned.

"Yeah, no, I just...it's nothing. I probably imagined it."

"Astra!" A deep male voice called out.

A smiling Jason Bishop waved his hand high above the crowd.

I turned away.

"Astra!" he called again, louder this time.

Emma and Alice turned to look.

Emma whistled. "Oh, my. Please tell me he's single," she said. With a wide-eye glance, she added, "And human. Ooh, he's sweaty. I like them sweaty."

"Stop it, Emma." I cringed, but turned and put a bright smile on my face. "Hey, Jason!" I called back and waved. Whispering, I warned Emma to be nice. "He's a middle school teacher."

Now, to be clear: I waved.

Lifted my hand up, palm forward, and swung my arm side to side to return the greeting. I did not lift my hand up, palm facing back, and swing my hand back and forth in the universal motion that said, "come here."

But "come here" he did.

"Hey there!" he said. "Ladies," he added, nodding toward Emma and Alice. That boyish grin would've lit up my life from the inside out if I wasn't already immune to the charms of men.

Entirely.

I said it. I meant it.

Emma and Alice moved forward, closer to my side.

"Hi, Jason. Nice to see you," I said.

Waving to my apparent wing-women, I

introduced the two to the handsome middle school teacher. After politely mopping off the copious amounts of sweat with a towel, Jason shook everyone's hand.

"I waited for you the other morning, Astra, hoping you and your younger sister would continue joining me for that morning run," he said with a long look. "Did Ayla have a really tough time recovering from the soreness?"

Ayla had been lying on a couch complaining for four days running now.

Yet she'd gotten in her closet remarkably fast when a murderer broke into the house. I mean, for someone in so much pain.

"I think she's playing it up for dramatic effect, if you want to know the truth." I smiled. "I don't know that I'm going to get her back out any time soon."

Jason laughed heartily.

"Anyway," I continued. "Sorry to have missed you. I got caught up in a case Emma and I had," I told him, gesturing toward the detective without elaborating. "I'll probably start running again in a day or two after we wrap up. I've been staying up pretty late, so it's been hard to get up early." Because of vampires. But we'll leave that part out.

"I'm glad it wasn't me you were avoiding,"

Jason responded, his eyes twinkling mischievously. Then he winked.

Emma's eyebrow raised.

Before I could say anything to him, or punch Emma in the face for that stupid eyebrow, Jason cleared his throat and bowed slightly. "If you ladies will excuse me, I'm in dire need of a shower and something to eat. Alice, Emma." He paused. "Astra."

As he walked away from us, I felt the back of my neck burn.

"What the hell was that about?" Emma asked. "Spill the tea, girlfriend."

I glared at her. "He was just being nice."

"Nice? You're kidding, right?" Emma put her hands on her hips. "That middle school teacher has some smoldering bedroom eyes, and they were—much to my disappointment—not on me. They were also not on Alice. They were on you, my dear. Are you seriously telling me you did not notice the bedroom eyes?"

"Cut it out, detective." I looked away from her incredulous glare. "I'm not looking for a relationship."

"I'm not saying you should. I'm saying you should let him take you out on a date or two."

"He didn't ask!"

"He will."

"I doubt it." I softened my tone, hoping to defuse her onslaught of dating advice. "Look, I'm not ready for a relationship. I just got home. I just got this owl. Just getting to know my sisters. This new job. Not ready."

"How old are you again?" Emma asked.

"Thirty-three."

"Wow, have you considered therapy?" Emma's eyebrows shot up.

I frowned. "I don't need therapy! Holy crow, get all the way off my back, would you? Just because I'm not entertaining a relationship with a guy that hasn't asked me out, and who I've seen exactly twice in my entire life, I need therapy?"

"I didn't say you did." She rolled her eyes. "I just think you have a lot of unresolved issues—"

"Maybe I do!" I told her hotly. "And maybe I'll work through them in my own time, okay?"

"Okay, okay." Emma held her hands up in surrender. "He's hot. And he seems interested. That's all I'm saying." I glared. "That's all I'm saying!"

"How about you not say anything else?"

She didn't.

But she did hum "Hot for Teacher" by Van Halen.

MY MOTHER HOSTED a dinner to celebrate the end of the case.

Since this was only the second star card case, I was afraid a festival dinner and wrap-up had just become a "thing" we would have to do from now on.

That's how paranormal rituals get started, you know. You do something twice, and suddenly, it's a freaking tradition.

I tried to argue, but my mother was insistent that "we have to thank the goddess for her help with the case, for trusting us to set things right, and have a formal ritual of conclusion, dear."

We did that in the military.

We just did it in the pub.

With a beer.

Okay, more than one beer.

Pistachio and Alice attended. The chieftain was beaming, smitten to the core that Alice was by his side. As cynical as I was about relationships, even I found it sweet.

Detective Emma Sullivan sat alone at the center of attention, my sisters and Alice peppering her with questions about Meryl Hawkins and the intricacies of the plan to steal millions of dollars and an entire company utilizing a vengeful, tempestuous pixie.

"So Paul Wakefield had nothing to do with anything?" Althea asked while spooning more mashed potatoes onto her plate.

Emma shook her head. "Orlando's dropping the case. Meryl used his access to transfer the money, but it was in his bank account for less than a day. Ultimately, it went into her offshore account in the Cayman Islands."

"And what about Ebony?" my sister asked her.

Emma looked at Pistachio. "Did the seer know about Amethyst's plan?"

The chieftain shook his head. "Ebony has gone into seclusion to contemplate her role in this. She believed Amethyst and now realizes that she should have come and talked to me." He frowned. "Times are different. A male chieftain is not the norm, and I think everyone has to learn a new way to treat one another in this new era of...of—"

"Equality?" Ayla asked.

"Equity," Althea corrected.

"Freedom," Rex said quietly. The vampire sat at the table next to his sister, his plate empty. "We have all been granted freedom for the first time in many years. It is a new thing for most of us." He looked up. "Our tribes must learn how to exist within it and manage the new choices we've been given."

"Hear, hear," Pistachio said, holding up a piece of chocolate like a wine glass.

"And on that note, I have to pee," Emma told the table bluntly. She pushed her chair away and left the room.

"I like her," Ayla said with a smile. "She's cool for a human."

"We all like her, dear," Aunt Gwennie said. "Eat those Brussels sprouts."

"But I don't like them."

"Eat them anyway."

"Excuse me," Rex said shortly, pushing back his chair and heading in the direction his sister had just gone. I watched him curiously, wondering why he'd gone after her. Vampires didn't have to use the facilities the way everyone else did.

Archie, who was perched on a chair to my right, clicked his beak. I turned. His wide eyes stared into mine, and he turned his head swiftly down the hall. Confused, I leaned in. "You should go and listen," he said ominously.

"Excuse me," I murmured to the table, pushing away—earning a few odd glances as I left.

"Is there a secret meeting I don't know about?" Althea asked wryly.

I walked down the hall until I heard low voices coming from a closed door. It was the herb room. Why would they be in the herb room?

I stopped in front of it.

"You have to get away from them, Emma," Rex told his sister, his low voice hard. "This is a house full of witches. They are prominent, well known. Why didn't you tell me that you were working with the witch, best friends with her? You asked me questions like you were investigating some case, not auditioning for a new best bud," his angry voice hissed. "You don't know what forces you're dealing with!"

"I am not going to let you scare me into abandoning my friend," Emma responded, her voice tight with anger. "If I can have a vampire brother, I can have a witch best friend. You're completely overreacting."

"You don't know what they're capable of!" Rex's voice rose.

"I know that they won't hurt me. Not ever. I trust them." Emma's voice was sharp. "I care about them. Anyway, this isn't your choice, Rex. It's my life."

My mouth dropped open as I leaned against

the wall. I'd never sensed Rex felt like this about witches. About me.

"That girl in there is a threat to me. To us."

My blood ran cold.

First, because he called me girl.

Man, I hate that.

What did he think I would do to him? To Emma?

"You're not her enemy, Rex," Emma said forcefully. "And she isn't your enemy."

"Did you ever stop to think about the risks at all?" Rex growled. "You've got to get away from her. You don't even know what you're talking about. Look at what's happened to you the past few days! Murderous pixies, potion comas? Wake up, Emma! She's not some run-of-the-mill country-bumpkin witch. She's military-trained!"

"So am I, Rex. Enough." I could hear the echo of her resolve. When Rex didn't respond, she added, "She's right in there. Her family opened their home to us. Invited us to dinner. You're being crazy right now. Astra's my friend. And they accept you more than Mom and Dad, you know…look, just stop this."

"I'm not going back to Las Vegas," Rex said forcefully, his voice louder than usual. "If you can't use your brain enough to get away from the paranormal before it turns on you, then someone has to stay here and protect you from your own idiocy."

My eyes grew wide.

Well.

This should be fun.

THANK YOU FOR READING!

I hope you enjoyed Owl's Fair! Please think about leaving a review! Astra, Archie and the whole Arden family continue their adventures in Book 3, Magic's a Hoot!

KEEP UP WITH LEANNE LEEDS

Thanks so much for reading! I hope you liked it! Want to keep up with me?

Visit leanneleeds.com to:

Find all my books…

Sign up for my newsletter…

Like me on Facebook…

Follow me on Twitter…

Follow me on Instagram…

Thanks again for reading!

Leanne Leeds

FIND A TYPO? LET US KNOW!

Typos happen. It's sad, but true.

Though we go over the manuscript multiple times, have editors, have beta readers, and advance readers it's inevitable that determined typos and mistakes sometimes find their way into a published book.

Did you find one? If you did, think about reporting it on leanneleeds.com so we can get it corrected.

Made in the USA
Monee, IL
08 July 2022

99256267R00198